Christ____
at
Gilly Downs
Novella

EMMA LOMBARD

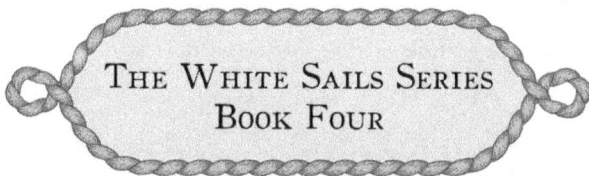

Come join the crew! Subscribe to my newsletter at www.EmmaLombardAuthor.com for fun giveaways and to receive advance notice about future book releases.

This book is dedicated to my team of loyal beta readers, without whom this novella would not have seen light. Thank you for requesting this encore—this one's for you!

AUTHOR'S NOTE

This novella has a slightly different format to the first three books in The White Sails Series. Firstly, it's a novella, and secondly, it captures the points-of-view of several of the characters from the series, as opposed to only Seamus and Grace's points-of-view.

It's a snapshot in time that jumps forward ten years after *Grace Arising* (The White Sails Series Book 3). Discover what your favourite characters have been up to, and join in the celebration as everyone reunites for a Christmas at Gilly Downs.

Chapter One

SEAMUS FITZWILLIAM

CLIFFVIEW COTTAGE, DARLING POINT, 16 DECEMBER 1853

7 AM.

Mentally running through his tasks for the day, Seamus glanced out of the dining-room window. The low-hanging clouds offered scant reprieve to the run of recent scorching summer days. Christ, not even seven in the morning and his shirt was already clinging to his back. The clamminess that preceded summer storms in the colony was worse than the sun's dry, blistering heat.

This morning's meeting with Captain McKay on the *Saviour of the Seas* would be a muggy affair. He was looking forward to securing the passenger manifest to pick out the family men. Gilly

Downs was in desperate need of shepherds, shearers and general hands, but all the unmarried men had scarpered after dreams of gold. He hoped the men yoked with wives and children would be glad of a secure position on Victor Shyling's property, especially with the decent wages on offer.

The dining-room's mustard walls were cheery, decorated with various colonial landscapes gifted to them by Dr Sykes over the years. The doctor had always had a knack with paint, and the oil paintings reflected the sunburnt earth's reds and golds. The air was thick with the smell of rain, coffee, and freshly baked bread. Breakfast smells. Family smells. Seamus jolted as Grace's butter knife clattered to her plate, the ping cold and brittle, its creamy blade leaving a smear of oil on the table cloth. She was recovering well from a mild case of influenza—then again, Sykes had armed her with enough potions to rival an apothecary.

"Good grief!" she exclaimed through a stuffy nose. She swept aside Edwin's blonde hair, revealing the blackened scab running up the lobe of his ear. "I still can't believe Mr Ridley did this to you."

"What did you say this time?" Emily asked, one blonde brow cocking up just like his own did.

"I didn't do anything!" Edwin pursed his lips, the dark fuzz on his top lip framing his displeasure. Seamus resolved to show the boy how to shave after breakfast. It would be less of a baptism of fire than his first time under the tutelage of a fellow midshipman, who had only begun shaving himself two months prior. The inexperienced guidance, rolling ship deck, and lethally sharp blade had resulted in a massacre that had earned him a good-humoured ridiculing by the officers for his close shave with death.

"That's not entirely true," countered Seamus. He shuffled his bottom back on the polished oak seat, un-upholstered but sturdy. With the band of pain tightening across his forehead, he stiffened as Grace scowled darkly from across the breakfast table, challenging him.

"Surely you can't sanction our son nearly having his ear ripped off, no matter the transgression?" she said, her face the red of autumn foliage.

"I gave no cheek, Father!" objected Edwin through gritted teeth, the edges of his lips white with displeasure.

Edwin's formal address sent a twinge of longing stabbing through Seamus's chest, a longing for a boyhood now passed. The father in him also swelled with pride, watching Edwin take one step further towards manhood. Despite this growing maturity, he had been resolute his boy would not step aboard any of their vessels until he had completed all his studies. A fact he had used to console Grace all these years at her concern that once Edwin stepped aboard a ship, his contact with them would be minimal. It was highly illogical of her to want to keep him pressed close at such an age, but they had already lost one son, and he understood her reluctance to bid another farewell. However, the time was nearly upon them, and she needed to cut the apron strings. Mollycoddling the lad now would not ready him for a life aboard a ship.

Seamus studied his simmering son, and firmed his voice. "Tell your sister the truth of it, young man."

"We were lined up for class, completely silent. Hodgeson was kicking the back of my shoes. I turned to glare at him, though I never uttered a sound. Mr Ridley hauled me out of line by my ear, and marched me to his office. Received a dozen cane strokes across my palms too." Edwin's eyes shone bright blue in the aftermath of his defence.

Seamus nodded pragmatically. "I'd say you've learned your lesson not to break rank, even when lining up for class."

"Seamus!" Grace's voice was sharp, almost shrill. "It is the Australian College —a boys' school—*not* a ship full of naval sailors."

Seamus lay his fists on either side of his plate, his half-eaten scrambled eggs and bacon forgotten. Raising his voice would only fan her smouldering maternal instinct, a force he had learned long ago he was powerless against. Scooping a remnant of salty bacon from inside his cheek with his tongue, he swallowed it, and lowered his register. "Edwin's a man. He needs an understanding of a man's world. He'll cross paths with many a Mr Ridley in life. The sooner he learns how to deal with the likes of him, the better."

"Poppycock! If you shan't go to the school to protest this, *I will*." She vehemently slathered more butter on her toast.

Seizing his knife and fork, he attacked the congealing egg on his plate, the rich, creamy warmth from earlier now cold and rubbery. "If Edwin is to succeed in captaining his own vessel one day, he *must* learn the rigours of good discipline." He chewed more vigorously than the soft, savoury texture warranted, then took a deep mouthful of lukewarm coffee to wash it down. "Besides, I already paid Mr Ridley a visit yesterday. I went to establish the man's take on discipline, quite believing we shared the same ideals."

The colour in Grace's smooth cheeks lessened, and she straightened in her chair, the bosom of her blouse stretching and flashing a glint of gold from her Luckenbooth brooch. "And do you?"

"Not particularly. Turns out that Ridley doesn't favour the attention given to what he termed, *this rabble of colonial backwater brats*." Seamus drew his brows together in recollection. "He reckons they're all-pervading and unstoppable—like brambles. Says it's a result of these colonial boys having breathed the free air of individuality too early, effectively making it impossible to enforce their compliance. He also rambled on about the solid institutionalised discipline of a good old British grammar school, and how sorely lacking it is in the colony."

"Such harsh corporal punishment for minor infractions is

unwarranted. I hope you set him straight on the matter?" Grace bit into her marmalade-laden toast like a snapping turtle.

Seamus tightened his brow. "Harm and discipline are two separate matters, Dulcinea. While I disagree with Ridley that children adopt a sense of devotion to compliance when whipped, it would be remiss of me to coddle our son. I'm duty-bound to equip him for the world."

Grace swiped the corners of her tight lips with the linen napkin. "I didn't mean for him to be coddled—"

Emily's teaspoon rattled in her saucer. "Cappy! Mamam! *Please*! Must you squabble so?" Her flushed neck pivoted between Grace and Seamus, her chin set in objection.

Whereas he tended to retreat into himself during conflict—and Grace was inclined to express all her emotions with a furious blush and a verbal outburst—in her twenty-one years, Emily had learned to neatly balance a combination of the two. She had his ability to keep her emotions in check, Grace's verbal articulation, and her own natural inclination to thoroughly disarm people with her smile. Ever the eternal peacekeeper, she flashed a grin at her brother. "Is Eddy not ready to begin his training aboard the *Elias* under Captain Hunt? You were twelve when you started your naval career, weren't you, Cappy? Eddy is already sixteen."

Seamus clinked the silver cutlery together on the empty plate, pondering his daughter's intelligent reasoning. "I was indeed. Except that Edwin isn't heading into a career with the Royal Navy." He swung his head toward Edwin, narrowing his eyes. "To be a successful merchant master, it's essential you first learn the commercial subjects of accounts and bookkeeping—to prepare for a life of business."

"Which I've done, sir," said Edwin. "Mamam and Mr Hicks have been teaching me all the ins and outs of shipping, and importing and exporting."

This was true. Every Saturday, for over two years, Edwin had attended his apprenticeship at the Elias Shipping Company.

Hicks had taken Edwin under his wing, shown him how to meticulously record passenger manifests to account for all new arrivals on their ships, calculate taxes on imported goods to ensure the governor was not getting more than his fair share, and complete the myriad of paperwork required for each voyage. Seamus had invited Edwin to meetings with pastoralists to learn how to negotiate shipping costs that left both parties pleased with the fairness of the deal. Everything Seamus taught Edwin, he taught him to do better, and with a seriousness of purpose. He made the lad think about the consequences of his actions, which meant the boy was not as carefree as his sister. Though this was not necessarily a dilemma, and Seamus was delighted with the promise Edwin showed. In fact, he might even go as far as to say that after years of commercial tutelage, his son was even beginning to appreciate the path he was on.

Seamus nudged his empty plate away, and rested his clasped hands on the table edge, his thumb toying with his scarred wrist. "Despite your personal discord with Mr Ridley, his school employs the best there is in the Southern Hemisphere. Your Drawing Master, John Wright, was apprenticed with Jim Buchanan at Arrowsmith Cartographers in London before his posting out here. It's only by virtue of the man's weak lungs that he left London to seek a better climate here in Sydney Town. Wright's mind is as sharp as a razor, and his extensive reputation for the neatness and finished style of his maps precedes him. You couldn't do better, even in London. And that Mr Winters is a thoroughly qualified and experienced businessman."

"If he's such an astute businessman, what's he doing stuck teaching in a backwater hole like Sydney Town? Why isn't he off making his fortune?" retaliated Edwin. In perfect imitation of Seamus, he too pushed his empty plate away and calmly clasped his hands, remaining just as still and solemn.

Seamus bit down on his molars, but he took a steady breath. "Mr Winters retired from business, and passed his enterprise over to his son. You're fortunate the man adopted the role as Head of the Mercantile Department in order to impart his knowledge to you lot."

Edwin folded his arms across his chest, looking so much like Grace did when she wanted to be obeyed. "Our Em's right. I'm old enough to take a position aboard a ship. By your own admission, Father, you've supported my apprenticing under Mr Hicks these past few years. Just imagine what I could accomplish in London with Mr Delisle?"

The boy's argument was sound, but Seamus was not about to let him believe he had won. Not just yet. What his son lacked in height, he made up for with a mind too wise for his years. Grace's face tightened and paled in realisation. No, he would not concede to his son's demands before easing his wife into acceptance first. Edwin would leave Australia one day, whether she liked it or not. He would have to persuade her to see that the fierce independence she had sewn into their children all these years was now coming to fruition. He was damned proud of his boy's determination!

"By rights, you should be preparing for your final drawing exam next week," said Seamus.

"It's more practical than theoretical," explained Edwin.

"In that case, I'm meeting with Captain McKay this morning to discuss the *Saviour*'s passenger manifest. It would behove you to shadow him for the next couple of days. Learn the myriad of preparations required upon arrival in port. I'm also dining with him aboard the ship this evening. Hicks was supposed to join me, but since he's indisposed by personal matters, you may sup with us instead."

Edwin's shoulders drew back, and his lips twitched up. "Thank you, sir."

Emily interjected, "On the topic of apprenticeships, I suppose now is as good a time as any to tell you that after four long years, I've completed mine." She shuffled upright under Seamus's renewed interest, smiling at him, and not with the professional, tight-lipped smile Edwin had given him, but with a genuine wide-mouthed grin.

Seamus ignored Edwin tweaking a mischievous eyebrow at his sister, dipping his head in thanks for diverting the conversation from him. Emily had won all the awards and certificates for her dressmaking efforts at Madame Dubois's school. Madame had put Emily forward to her friend, Mrs Moore, whose Pitt Street dress shop was the talk of the town.

Emily flourished her hands, communicating as much with gestures as with words. "Mrs Moore no longer wants my talent wasted on fashioning undergarments and sewing buttons as an apprentice. I'm now responsible for the embroidery on Mrs Deas Thomson's new gown. Mrs Moore says I could design gowns in Paris with my skill."

Paris? Seamus pressed his clasped knuckles to his mouth, humming thoughtfully. "Not a terrible notion." He leaned over and ran his thumb down Emily's warm cheek. "So long as you're only making the gowns and not modelling them. There is a line of modesty one must not cross."

Emily's eyes sparked feverishly at his cautionary tone. "Mrs Moore holds dances in her shop, once a month on a Saturday. She clears out the whole back room for the selectively fashionable to come and show off their fancy footwork in our latest gowns."

"Darling, I doubt you'll be afforded the same privileges as Mrs Moore's paying clientele." His voice was light with amusement. "Still, there's no finer place for you to continue your education of the wider world."

Scrunching her napkin into a ball, Grace smiled at Emily. "I suppose there are worse things in the world to be than a dressmaker. It'll certainly be a handy practicality once you have a family."

"Oh no, Mamam," declared Emily earnestly. "I don't plan on

only making corsets and children's clothes. I take my role as Mrs Moore's first hand completely seriously. I'll design the finest gowns for Sydney Town's gentry. When the world hears of my designs, I'll be whisked away to London to create the latest fashions."

The creaking floorboard announced Sally McGilney's approach as she burst into the conversation with her usual bluster. "Them's mighty grand notions you've got there, Miss Emily. Might even end up sewing a frock or two for the Queen of England 'erself!"

Seamus harrumphed. "When *will* Mrs Moore cease trying to draw a societal season to life here in Sydney Town? The seasons of London and Paris were left at their respective docks when their citizens flocked halfway around the world to start anew here."

Grace chuckled, the motion softening her eyes. "I doubt the nouveau riche of New South Wale's grazing aristocracy are about to resurrect *those* social nuances. Besides, it's far too hot to be flouncing around in layers of silk!" She laughed freely at their daughter's scowl.

Heavens above, he never tired of hearing the happiness in his wife's voice.

Grace gave Emily's hand a conciliatory pat. "With the men away this evening, what say you and I sup at the Australian Hotel? It's been an age since we did that."

McGilney slid the coffeepot onto the white linen without spilling a drop, and the hearty aroma of fresh coffee wafted across to Seamus's nostrils, perfuming the summer breeze. He poured himself a fresh cup as Emily perked up at Grace's words.

"Yes, please! Will you meet me at Mrs Moore's after closing? We can stroll over to the hotel—if it's not raining." Emily cast a baleful look at the low-hanging clouds out the window.

Grace squeezed her hand. "Perfect! Five-thirty it is then."

Dutifully clearing the dirty plates, the housekeeper delicately balanced the crockery on a tray. A practical woman, McGilney had been terribly heavy-handed when she first joined the household back in Abertarff House in London. Many a china plate had met its fate in the early days. Initially sceptical of the rough-edged words that tumbled from her mouth like cracked pebbles, Seamus was relieved that time had tempered her manners. She had earned his favour and become the children's favourite. Grace, of course, had always had a soft spot for her being Lambert McGilney's sister.

"Thank you, McGilney," he said.

The housekeeper nodded her brown-bun at him, automatically bobbing in a curtsey. Balancing the tray's corner on the table edge, she drew a packet from her apron pocket, and turned to Grace. "Nearly forgot. A letter for you, marm. Big Bob delivered it this morn. Looks like it's from Gilly Downs." McGilney beamed as she wiped her hand over the hip of her skirt. "I'd recognise milady's writin' any day. Not that I can read, mind. But 'er words all 'as them swirly tails." Taking a deep breath, she babbled on, "It don't feel too plump. Can't be much news in it. As my Gilly used to say, letters is like beans on toast, all grand at first 'til they spill ill tidings. O'course, if 'tisn't bad news, then it's back to being beans on toast. He were a wise lad that brother o' mine!"

By Neptune, the woman would talk underwater given half a chance!

McGilney headed towards the door with the fully laden tray, swinging backwards to bump the door open with her backside. Her dark brown eyes widened, "Suppose milady'll be tellin' you all about that maid of hers. Little trollop got herself in a right fix she did." Her scandalous huff followed her into the hallway like a faithful dog.

Grace's slender fingers made short work of messily ripping the envelope. Seamus sucked in a sharp breath. No matter how many times over the years he had offered the merits of how a neatly slit envelope gave a letter a safe place to return to once read, she always tore them to pieces in her excitement to extract the contents.

Grace scoured the page, her friend's words clearly doing wonders to revive her humour now that the conversation had been steered away from Edwin's departure. She glanced up and grinned. "Before anyone is whisked anywhere, I've some splendid tidings." The worried mother disappeared as the smile returned to her green eyes. "Adelia has invited us all to spend Christmas at Gilly Downs."

"How marvellous!" Emily lay her napkin on the table. "Excuse me from the table, please?" Seamus nodded, and she rose, glancing out the window again. "Do you think it'll rain today?" She nibbled her bottom lip in contemplation and directed her next question at Seamus. "Should I water Alby's hibiscus bush before I set off to work?"

"An extra dousing won't do it any harm," Seamus said. Emily's fondness for her carapace-capering friend had only grown over the past eighteen years. Since she shouldered full responsibility for the creature, he could not bemoan its presence in the garden below. The palatial enclosure was ample for its solitary monarch, who spent most of the day sleeping anyway. At nearly two hundred pounds, the tortoise's days of being carried around were long gone, but it did not stop Emily dutifully calling on him every morning like a royal subject.

"I suppose he's always got his prickly pears," Emily said. "You know how he loves those!"

Seamus chuckled and shook his head. "That tortoise has a better life than most of human inhabitants in this town."

Emily theatrically thrust her nose in the air, and flicked her loose curls over her shoulder with her hand. "And rightly so! He has better manners than most!"

Chapter Two

TOBY HICKS

STRAWBERRY HILL, SYDNEY TOWN, 16 DECEMBER 1853

9 AM.

Gripping his son's chubby thighs slung over his shoulders, Toby swung his head, admiring the quaint village of Strawberry Hill. Dotted throughout the scrubby, dry paddocks, quaint cottages like his, and the occasional mansion, were linked by sandy tracks trying awfully hard to be streets. Most were straight, some as crooked as a corkscrew. It was only a half-hour walk to town from here, but Toby preferred the solitude. Village life offered a different world to the bustling wave of humanity down the hill.

"Down, Pa! I want to see Mam," gushed Lucas.

Asking his four-year-old son to settle down was akin to asking a fire not to burn. Swinging Lucas from his shoulders with a laugh, Toby planted a noisy kiss on the compact, rosy cheek—inhaling the intoxicating scent of pure love. He followed the little boy into the cottage, ducking below the low lintel. He breathed in the homely smells of wood ash, broth and ale. The weighty wicker basket in the crook of his arm spelled the success of his early morning venture out to the market, and he deposited it on the flagstone floor.

"Quietly, Lucas. Your mam and the new babe might be asleep." He grinned at his boy. The family resemblance leaned heavily towards the Hicks side, and Lucas was a mirror image of Toby's younger brother, Shelby, at this age. From broad shoulders to the sandy mop to the grey eyes that sparkled with a boldness missing from Toby's own childhood. It was a blessing his boy was not crippled by his own lack of confidence, and he certainly was not planning on crushing the boy's spirits with fists or boots, as his father or that stumpy-legged Cook Phillips had him.

A hum of curiosity vibrated through the youngster's small, square back as he peered down at the covered basket on the floor. "Can I take Mam her 'nana?"

Toby nodded.

With his milk teeth clenched in a delighted grin, Lucas lifted the cloth edge. "Pomegranates, plums, apri-tots." He stabbed each fruit as he named it, then inhaled sharply as he held the curved, yellow fruit up in triumph. "And 'nanas! I like 'nanas."

"Me too," Toby whispered, hunching his shoulders to his ears like it was their little secret. "A special treat. One of those is for Mam."

Lucas grabbed two of Toby's fingers in his pudgy hand, and dragged him towards the cottage's rear. "Come, Pa."

Toby laughed again at the little boy's enthusiasm, and let himself be led towards the bedchamber door. Little blighter was surprisingly strong! "Just a minute, young man." He knocked, and a muffled voice called out from the silence beyond. He opened the door a crack, carefully peering around. "All safe to enter?"

Maggie, the maid, handed a neatly swaddled bundle to Erin in the bed. Over at the table before the window, Dr Sykes snapped the brass clasps of his black bag shut, and beckoned with his dark head. "Hicks, come on in. Meet your new daughter."

Toby stopped, his fingers slipping free of Lucas's at the sight of his bloodless, limp-haired wife. For the love of God, she looked as though she barely had the strength to blink, let alone hold a newborn. Oblivious to his mother's condition, Lucas reattached his grip to Toby's fingers and hauled him over to the bed, grunting with the effort. The youngster clambered onto the bed beside Erin, and with a touching delicacy, lay a possessive hand on his sister's dark, fuzzy head.

"Who's dis?" he asked.

Erin smiled and scooped her free arm around Lucas. "This is Dorothy. Your new sister."

"Doffy? I's a big brother?" He beamed, looking between Erin and Toby.

"You are indeed, my boy." Toby smiled gently at Erin, hoping he hid his worry at the sight of her green almond eyes, too large above her pronounced cheekbones. He planted a gentle kiss on Erin's rumpled hair. She smelled of the salty remnants of sweat, birth waters, and blood, all scents of exhaustion. He gripped her hand. Good God, she was all skin and bone! His mind darted back to the first time he had kissed her hand, feeling the fineness of her bones through the white lace glove. He had marvelled at the loveliness of it, but there was nothing lovely about *this* intimate acquaintance with her skeleton.

He knew her confinement had not been easy, but he was unaware just how gravely ill she must have been to become this dangerously thin. He leaned in to peer at his daughter's tiny face. "Hello Dorothy," he whispered, a pang of nostalgia opening a flood of memories of Lucas at his birth. He had been just as pink and perfect.

Toby flicked his gaze to Erin's pale face, and smiled cautiously. "I bought a basket of fruit." He bobbed his head towards the kitchen. "Thought it would be easy eating." He stroked the soft whorls of Dorothy's minute ear—he had a fondness for the velvety softness of a newborn's ear, that delicate whorl of nature's perfection, like a seashell. "There's also an apple and rhubarb pie from Sally McGilney."

"How thoughtful." Erin swayed gently as the bundle in her arms mewled.

Beaming at his mother, Lucas thumped her banana on the bedcover and immediately bit the top of his own, grimacing at the hard peel's crunch.

Erin laughed lightly at his antics, and cracked the banana open along the neat perforation his teeth had made.

"I do it," demanded Lucas, yanking back the fruit. He peeled off the remaining skin, tongue clamped between his teeth in concentration. Dropping the peel to the bedcover, he took a giant bite, his cheeks bulging like a winter squirrel.

Maggie scooped Lucas off the bed, groaning in jest as she hauled his solid body. "Right-ho, wee man," she said in her cheerful Irish accent. "'Tis time for yer weekly bath." Depositing the giggling child on the floor, she patted his bottom playfully, nudging him towards the door. "Outside with ye. I'll fetch some hot water to warm yer bucket." She glanced at Sykes. "Perhaps the good doctor might like some tea and a slice of pie?"

Sykes tucked his hat under his elbow, and slid his bag off the table with a nod. "Won't say no. Might you prepare the same for Mrs Hicks?" He raised his black brows at Erin.

Erin nodded wearily, her tongue darting out to moisten her

chapped lips with little success. Toby swallowed thickly in sympathy.

"Yes, sir." Maggie bobbed, and guided Lucas out with a hand on his head.

Obediently, the little boy toddled towards the door, looking back at Erin expectantly. "I come back after my bath?"

"Yes, sugar plum," said Erin, her dark sunken eyes blinking slowly.

Dr Sykes shut the door quietly behind him. Discarding the banana peel on the bedside table, Toby eased himself beside his wife. "Long night?" he whispered.

"Long one for you too. You should've slept instead of sitting vigil over me."

"Once you've your strength back, how about I take you for a picnic to our beach?" He stroked her forehead with his thumb, teasing back the moist strands of hair.

She hummed, closing her eyes as she smiled. "I remember that day as though it were yesterday."

So did he, the memory of it opening like a spring bloom invited by the sun. He had been single-minded about wooing the pretty Miss Lissing, who was an undiscovered mystery he was determined to solve. Emboldened by the success of their first outing to the Sunday cricket, he had hired a horse and buggy, and invited her on a picnic. The school's white-painted door swung open, and Erin stood before him in a pretty salmon gown that matched the pink flush in her cheeks.

He bounded up the front steps. "Your servant, madam," he said, bowing deeply.

She eyed the small buggy and smiled, "I see I'll be riding in style today."

"Of course." He grinned. "Only the best for my lady."

She sat beside him on the wide padded seat, arranging her skirts and tying her bonnet's black, silk ribbons. Popping open a parasol that matched the colour of her gown, she glanced shyly at him from the corner of her eye. "Where are we going?"

"Out of town. For a picnic. I spotted a pretty little beach as the *Elias* approached the Heads. It's a wondrous paradise that will fade into drabness once your dainty foot touches it."

"Oh, it's like that, is it?" She raised a cheeky eyebrow. "My presence will cast a dreary shadow over the place." She sighed deeply, and turned her head from him.

A stab of realisation pierced Toby's innards with a pain as true as being run-through with a broadsword. His cheeks heated violently in mortification that his flippancy had been so misunderstood. "Oh, God, no! I didn't mean it so! Forgive me. I should not attempt to be poetic with my words. I'm an inarticulate fool."

Her head whipped around, the handle of her parasol knocking her bonnet skew as she nudged him with her shoulder. "No, no, Toby. I shouldn't mock, even in jest. Especially when you're being so earnest. So romantic. I shouldn't have feigned indignation like that. I'm sorry."

Face still tight with embarrassment, Toby looked pointedly at the comely, red-faced woman next to him. Seeing her awkwardness matching his, he released the frown that drew his eyebrows together, and smiled bashfully. "Perhaps we should agree to speak plainly with one another, and leave the art of seduction to those with gilded tongues?"

"Absolutely! I couldn't agree with you more," said Erin, straightening her bonnet. They rode on in silence as the town's buildings were replaced by towering gum trees.

Toby cleared his throat nervously. "So, you think I'm romantic?"

Erin's back stiffened a little at the direct question, but heeding their agreement to speak plainly with one another, she nodded and flashed her neat white teeth. "I do. You're the first gentleman who has ever whisked me away to a tropical beach for a picnic. How much more romantic can one get?" Toby rolled his shoulders back smugly as she placed her hand on his arm. "If you don't find me dreary, does that mean you find me beautiful?"

Toby swallowed so deeply he was sure she could hear the gulp. He shifted the reins to one hand, and placed his hand over hers. "Erin Lissing, of all the beauties I've witnessed around the world, you are by far the most exquisite."

Erin shuffled closer to him so that their hips and shoulders pressed together, and Toby thought he might topple from the driver's seat with pleasure.

"I rather fancy this plain-talking, don't you?" she said.

Toby steered the buggy off the rutted track, pulling the horse to a halt under the spreading canopy of a heavy foliaged tree. Before his courage failed him, he grasped her tiny waist and eased her down. She surprised him by concentrating hungrily on his lips. Encouraged by her unblinking stare, Toby bent to kiss her. The edge of her bonnet nudged his cap, tipping it backwards and setting him off course, his lips ending up on her chin. Caught in another moment of awkwardness, he withdrew, laughing, relieved that she did the same.

Toby ran his hand across his hot nape and chuckled. "Appears I'm in desperate need of practice in *this* department too." He picked up his tweed cap, slapping it against his thigh to shake off the dust.

"Well then," said Erin, smiling sweetly. Sashaying her hips, she sauntered into the thicket of coastal shrubbery. "We'd best get going to your secluded little beach as quickly as possible so we may begin practising."

Toby watched her walk past a low bush, her skirts catching on the twigs. He slung a pack on his back, and slid the picnic basket from beneath the buggy seat. "Um, Erin?"

She stopped and turned. "Yes?"

Toby pressed his lips together, holding back a laugh as he pointed in the opposite direction. "Beach is this way."

It didn't take them long to break free of the dense vegetation. He smiled as Erin stopped at the sight of the tiny sandy cove flanked by a large flat rock on one side and rougher boulders on the other. The sand between the rocky outcrops was dazzlingly white, as fine as ground salt. Through the vivid aquamarine water, Toby spotted the rocky shelf's contours spreading into the ocean. It must have ended abruptly because there was a distinct line where the water became the dark-blue of deep water. A spectacular brigantine in full sail cut across his vision.

"Oh, Toby! It's magnificent!" She clasped a lace-gloved hand to her chest, her head turning in every direction as she absorbed the tranquillity and beauty.

Leaving her to admire the view from the grassy knoll, Toby stepped onto the sand and withdrew a sheet of new canvas from his knapsack. With some cajoling, and a bottle of Cape brandy, Sailmaker Mayer had let him borrow some new canvas from the *Elias*. Positioning the red-and-white-check covered wicker basket on the canvas, he stepped back to the grassy wedge. Without warning, he scooped the schoolmistress in his arms. She shrieked in delight, clinging to his neck as he carried her over the soft sand and deposited her onto the clean, white sail.

"Don't want you filling your pretty boots with sand, now do we?"

She sat down, curling the boots in question beneath her skirts. "Actually," she said, running her fingers through the sand. "I plan to dispose of my boots altogether, and bury my feet in the sand. It's so warm and fine."

She jumped as Toby dropped to his knees before her. "Allow me?" He grinned merrily as his words brought a furious blaze to her cheeks. Untucking her legs, she placed them straight out in front of her and leaned back on her arms, amusement lighting her almond eyes.

Her breath caught as his hands disappeared up the hem of her skirt, tracing along the bootlaces. His fingertips briefly brushed the smooth silk of her stocking before finding the lace's bow. He locked eyes with her as his hidden hands untied and unhooked the tiny ropes deftly and expertly. He tugged at the heel, and the first boot slid off effortlessly. Languidly repeating the exercise, he soon had her other boot off. Toby sat back on his heels, his hands resting on his thighs as he looked down at her tiny stockinged feet.

She wiggled her toes. "I shan't feel much with stockings on."

It was Toby's turn to inhale sharply as he took in the creamy skin of her décolletage, the firm round mounds of her breasts, and her impossibly tiny waist clenched in before the swell of her hips. Gingerly, he placed both his hands on the top of her left foot.

Her pupils widened, and her nostrils flared as she inhaled in anticipation. He ran his palms slowly up the sides of her calf until he found the ribbons of her stockings just below her knee. Erin shivered. Judging by the sun's warmth beating his own back, he knew it was not from cold. Absurdly pleased with himself at invoking this desirous response in her, he tugged the silk laces. They slid undone with silky ease, and with an unfamiliar gentleness, he rolled the smooth material down her warm leg. Her skin prickled beneath his fingertips. He stared at her bare toes, with nails neatly trimmed, skin so soft and clean—the rose-soap perfume evidence of a recent scrubbing. He slowly raised her foot, kissing her toes. Her skirt slid back slightly, revealing the fine pale hairs on her shin. Heartened that she had not stopped him, he planted light kisses along the arch of her foot and around her ankle. At this, Erin's gasp morphed into a whimper. With the greatest willpower he had ever had to exercise in his life, he gently set down her foot. Erin's mouth drooped in disappointment.

"Can't have your right foot getting jealous of your left, can I?" He winked. His own deep breaths sent blood pounding through his veins. He removed her other stocking with the same unhurried pace, stopping short of repeating the toe kissing. He did not trust himself to be able to stop at her ankle. Turning to busy his tingling hands, Toby drew the food from the basket. He had procured smoked mussels and a wedge of soft gouda. The crusty loaf was fresh from Mr Dortmund's bakery. He had paid a small fortune for the bottle of French Bordeaux from the wine merchant, but the occasion warranted it. Slicing some cheese and tearing off a chunk of bread crust, he handed it to Erin.

He bit down into his own, marvelling at the cheese's full, creamy flavour.

"I've had the finest French cheese on water biscuits before, but they don't come close to how extraordinarily delicious *this* is." Her narrow throat tightened as she swallowed a second bite. Her green, oval eyes studied him just as intently, their hue bright and glossy in the clear sunlight.

Toby moistened his lips. "For a lady of gentle breeding, you're the most enterprising and independent I've ever encountered. Voyaging to the other side of the world. Buying into a business partnership. All without the assistance of your father or a husband."

Erin's mouth softened, and she ran her hand down her own arm with a gentle stroke that suddenly gave Toby the ludicrous notion to want to be her arm at that very moment. Her lips curled coyly, her head tipping. "And do you like that about me?" She sipped at the glass of red wine he handed her. The tip of her pink tongue darted out to lick away the remnants of wine from her top lip.

Blinking to tear his stare from her rose-tinged mouth, he cast his gaze down to his own glass, and rolled the ruby liquid around the bulb, watching the wine slowly creep down the slick surface. Toby swallowed the half-chewed mouthful of bread and cheese in his mouth. The mass of improperly masticated food lodged dryly in his throat, and he quaffed a large mouthful of wine to dislodged the crust. "I do," came his minimal reply. "I like that a lot."

"I'm glad of your affection for me because I have the same for you."

Toby blinked in surprise at her bold words. "You do?"

Erin shuffled nearer and lay her head against his shoulder, fitting perfectly against him. "How could I not after witnessing your kindness and bravery—when you raced up the mainmast to help your brother through his first storm. Lord knows my heart jumped from my mouth at the thought of you falling. I could barely breathe for fear of it." She nuzzled closer, and sighed against his collarbone.

Toby tipped up her chin, bringing her near enough to feel her breath. He tugged her bonnet ribbon, and let the hat drop behind her with a sandy thud. He caressed her lips with his, and she responded instantly, kissing him back without hesitation.

Back in the darkened bedchamber in Strawberry Hill, Toby kissed those same lips, now dry and chapped. "I love you, my angel."

Erin dropped her head to his shoulder, and he scooped a hand around her summer-soft hair, and tucked her head snugly in the crook of his neck as he had that long-ago spring day.

"I'm that tired I could sleep for a thousand nights," she murmured.

Wishing he did not have to break the intimate moment, he reluctantly planted a kiss on her crown and eased off the bed, relieving her of the sleeping babe. "You do just that, sweetling. Young mademoiselle here can take her throne over here in the corner." He lowered the infant into the wicker bassinet. He pulled a sheet over his wife, the thin fabric sufficient covering for the muggy day. "I'll be in the kitchen with Dr Sykes." He nudged the small, silver bell on the bedside table within reach. "Ring if you need anything."

Sykes was still at the kitchen table, and Toby waved as he

made to rise. "Sit, sit, sit, Dr Sykes. We're long past that stage of ceremony, you and I." He smiled kindly.

"*You* sit before you fall, Hicks." Sykes nudged out the chair beside him with one foot.

"Won't say no," said Toby thickly as he ran his hands over his whiskers and tried for a deep breath to revive himself. Maggie slid a plate of rhubarb pie and a hot pot of dark, fragranced tea before him. He nodded in thanks as the maid cajoled his son through the front door to the iron tub outside.

"Tell me honestly, Sykes. How was it? She looks like she's been to hell and back." Watching Erin struggle through the night held the same horror as witnessing a wombat torn apart by dingoes, with him equally powerless to help. Pushing aside the pie, Toby took a long pull of scalding tea, relishing the comfort the hot drink always brought, and bracing for Sykes's words that might make this situation more real than the nightmare it was already.

"I won't varnish the truth, Hicks. You called for me just in time. There was a moment I thought I might lose her. Lose them both." His voice was as heavy as the prophecy. "She won't survive another like that. 'Tis a blessing the wee lassie came early and is on the smaller side. Next time, I recommend your wife loosen her stays and petticoat bindings, anything to ease the restriction on her already narrow pelvis."

Toby burst from his seat, the chair's wooden feet squealing on the stone. "There won't be a bloody next time if I can help it!" He had always thought her slenderness made her so lithe and graceful. Who knew her most endearing feature could be a death sentence? He snatched up the fire poker and stabbed the glowing logs in the hearth. With a satisfying crunch, one cracked in two, angrily spitting out a shower of sparks that landed at his feet, each glowing with one final flair of defiance before greying out. Jamming the poker back in its stand, he whirled on his heel. "What can I do for her now?"

Laying his fork across his empty plate, Sykes sighed heavily and leaned back in his chair. "I've no notion why birthing is so easy for some women and for others 'tis a death sentence. 'Tis a most vexing problem, and one for which I've yet to find a remedy." He drained the last of his tea. "In the meanwhile, she needs plenty of rest. And watch closely for childbed fever. It usually strikes a week to ten days during the lying-in."

"May I call on you at the first sign of fever?"

"Of course. Though I've been invited to join in the Christmas festivities at Gilly Downs, so send a fast rider to fetch me, if needs be."

"Ah, yes. We received the same invitation. Erin was so looking forward to it."

"Not possible now, I'm afraid."

"Never mind. I'll be here to keep watch over my wife. Captain Fitzwilliam granted me a couple of days off to celebrate our new arrival."

"Good." Sykes rummaged in his black bag at his feet. "Have your maid keep up a plentiful supply of caudle. She must add an egg yolk to the mixture of boiled wine and ground almonds. If you can't find almonds, breadcrumbs or oats will suffice." He placed a cork stoppered bottle on the table. "Add thirty drops of this meadowsweet tincture once a day. It'll aid in keeping the fever at bay." He scraped his long fringe back through his fingers. "But whatever you do, for God's sake, don't let those butchers at the rum hospital bleed her. That fool, Clarke, has everyone believing there's a danger in spicy caudles. Says they labour the heart and arterial system, but I disagree. New mothers require every assistance to build their strength in the aftermath." He rose from his seat, lifting his bag. "Now, if you'll excuse me, I've another patient to visit."

Chapter Three

BILLY SYKES

TELLER RESIDENCE, SYDNEY TOWN, 16 DECEMBER 1853

10.30 AM.

B illy stood before the mustard-coloured terrace house, and straightened his waistcoat after dismounting from his horse. Tethering the black gelding to the iron railing, he rubbed the white blaze on the horse's forehead as he glanced up at the balcony's brown, lattice ironwork. More interested in the new grass shoots that edged the low wall, the horse dipped his head out of Billy's reach, the bridle jangling impatiently.

It was Billy's favourite kind of weather in this burgeoning neighbourhood, a muggy, cloudy day when the sub-tropical sun relinquished its harsh mid-morning light to layers of grey. He stood still a moment longer, studying the new house before him. The drawing room glowed with flickering incandescence. A piano's delicate plink accompanying a cello's mournful wail was complemented by the honeyed tones of feminine singing. A woman in white reclined on a divan, somewhat veiled by the cerise cloak of draperies. The house flaunted an extravagant opulence that was rather alluring to a bachelor living a simple life above an apothecary.

Grace had tried for years to have him buy a cottage to set up a proper home, more so since he had retired as ship's surgeon and bought the apothecary from Ravensdale two years past. But he had never been able to bear the thought of the expense. His apothecary was thriving, and he was more than able to afford it. Despite Grace's protestations that charity began at home, he found himself offering his wares to the poorest Sydney Town had to offer, sometimes for nothing more than two eggs exchanged for a tincture, or the offer to darn his socks for a decoction. Husbandless mothers—widowed or otherwise—were his weakness. He had plenty of paying customers too, but they were a necessary means to a charitable end, and so he found himself still living in the large room above his shop.

The low, iron gate squeaked on its hinges as Billy stepped onto the narrow flagstone path. Beautiful heads of red flowers bloomed on voluminous bushes in the front garden, giving the place a distinctly tropical air. He paused a moment to appreciate the bright flowers, rubbing the frilly, yellow-edged petals that morphed into a deep red in the centre. Thin red fleshy stamens jutted out like an anemone's tentacles, their tiny yellow heads dusted with pollen. He sniffed the blossom, instantly rewarded with a light floral fragrance. Living above his apothecary meant he did not own the luxury of a garden, though if he did have one, he would very much like some of these magnificent blooms in it.

Releasing the object of curiosity, Billy climbed the two front steps, hesitating before knocking softly on the red-painted door. It opened a crack, revealing the curious face of a mob-capped maid. She smiled in recognition and swung the door open. Billy stepped into the narrow foyer, the main artery from which the downstairs rooms were connected, leading to a rear staircase.

"Good afternoon, Dr Sykes. Might I take your coat and hat, sir?"

"Thank you." Billy smiled, handing over his hat, and shrugging out of his coat.

"Mrs Teller is expecting you," said the fresh-faced girl, her eyes darting discretely to the ceiling.

Billy nodded in thanks, but a movement in the parlour to his right caught his eye. The music and singing stopped, and the graceful woman reclining on the divan rose, her loose, ink-black hair cascading down her back in a sleek waterfall. She was tall as he. The mesmerising topaz of her eyes halted his feet, but his glimpse was brief as she disappeared around the back of the door towards a male chuckle, her smile feline, those golden eyes mesmerising.

The private upstairs parlour was open-plan with a plush, floral lounge suite arranged prettily around the unlit fireplace. Fragrant hardwood was neatly piled in the hearth. The room was immaculately clean, and sprays of fresh flowers fluttered as though alive with butterflies, caressed by the bay breeze easing through the white French windows. Radiating pure feminine charm, the room was devoid of a *Mr* Teller's husbandly influence.

With a rustle of skirts, a finely dressed woman stepped into the room. Mrs Teller was in her late forties, but she was as striking and elegant as the first time he had laid eyes on her in his apothecary two years before. Her thick auburn hair was swept up on both sides by two long-toothed combs, emphasising her slim neck. Billy tried hard to keep his eyes on her delicately pointed chin, but it was impossible not to glance at her ample bosom. Mrs Teller noticed, and her lips twitched as she boldly fixed her gaze on his.

"Your servant, madam," said Billy, bowing low to avert his eyes.

"Dr Sykes." She flashed a neat row of white teeth between plump, rouged lips. "How good of you to make a personal delivery." She sauntered over, hips swaying with a mesmerising life of their own.

"Not at all, madam. 'Tis my pleasure." Billy flushed, handing over the brown package tied with string. Mrs Teller took it from him and, barely glancing at it, slid it onto the sideboard. She tilted her head, forcing him to look down at her.

"Tea, doctor?" she asked politely.

Despite usually priding himself on being an educated and articulate man, the best he managed was, "Er—ah—thank you."

"Or perhaps something stronger?"

"I—um—no, tea's grand."

Mrs Teller sashayed over to a small stove in the corner, where a small black kettle puffed silently. A shining polished tea set was already laid on a silver tray on the sideboard. Tilting at the hips, she leaned forward to busy herself with tea preparations, her skirts moulding around her pert backside. For the love of lilies, what a sublime derrière!

The teaspoon tinkled on the china, and Mrs Teller turned with a florally cup and saucer in hand. Billy's heart leapt into his mouth. She offered him the tea, her smile sucking the blood from his gut like a malnourished hookworm.

"Cat got your tongue, doctor?" She purred, unashamedly looking him up and down. The cup and saucer felt ridiculously tiny in his hand. Before he dratted-well fumbled and tipped the milky contents all over her elegant floral rug, he had best slide the saucer safely beside the brown package.

Ignoring her own cup of tea on the tray behind her, Mrs Teller gave him the same look she usually did during her monthly visits to the apothecary. The one that sent his heart skidding around his chest like an oiled piglet. The one that had made him decide on the spot that her home deliveries would not be relegated to his assistant.

"Why the stern face?" she asked, resting her hand lightly on her creamy décolletage. Billy fought the urge to glance down. Her voice was light and teasing. "You've quite a lovely smile when you use it, you know, doctor?"

"Not as lovely as yours, petal."

Humming, she took another step closer, and Billy was almost dizzy with the sweet feminine smell of her. "Isn't a woman alive who doesn't like to be told she's beautiful." Mrs Teller tilted her head again in that way that drained the saliva from his mouth. "So, you think me beautiful, Dr Sykes?"

"I—" She had an elegant nose, and beautiful, big blue eyes, and rosy, moist lips that he longed to kiss. *Get a hold of yourself, man. She's a patient!* She returned the frank look. A look too intimidating for him to hold, especially with the proximity of those ample breasts he tried so hard not to stare at. His throat squeaked. "You are *magnificent*."

Mrs Teller's tinkling laugh broke the intensity between them. "Takes a lot of work to get me looking like this. Doesn't come naturally, I assure you." Her laugh halted abruptly as she winced, and clutched the right side of her abdomen.

Billy scrunched his brow. "Are you in pain, Mrs Teller?"

She breezily flicked her manicured hand. "'Tis nothing your laudanum package can't fix."

Billy paused a moment, and then inclined his head at her. "Madam, I must point out that laudanum is for dulling the pain, not fixing the ailment. Will you permit me to examine you?" The instant the words were out of his mouth, a wave of heat swept his entire body. His offer was not out of the ordinary—he had examined thousands of patients in his lifetime. He opened his mouth to explain, but no sound emerged.

Mrs Teller's desirable lips curled tenderly, and she placed a hand on his chest. "How *thorough* an examination are we talking, Dr Sykes?" She reached a cool hand behind his neck and pulled him down for a slow, lingering kiss. He did not resist.

She tasted delicious, a delightful blend of salty and sweet! He pulled back, gasping at having not breathed through the entire kiss. How could he remember to respire with all his senses swimming like this?

Good God, she was a consummate professional! She plied her trade like none he had known before. A furious burn crept up from under his collar. Over the years he had prided himself on absolute discretion in this aspect of his life. Just because he had no time for wife did not mean the red-blooded male in him did not need attending. The straining tent of lust in his trousers was a clear betrayal of his youthful vow of chastity, broken many moons ago in a drunken night in port with Blight and O'Malley.

He had long given up indulging in knee-shakers in dingy alleys, realising there was far more pleasure to be had adoring a woman's body in the privacy of her bedchamber. He sensed Mrs Teller liked to be stroked and whispered to, that she enjoyed being kissed and loved. And God knew *what* this illogical affection was he felt for the woman before him? She was a regular at his apothecary and no stranger, yet he stood before her now in her parlour, trembling like a wet puppy.

"As thorough an examination as you'll allow, madam," he said, his cool and controlled tone not matching his heart's furious flailing.

There was no way Mrs Teller could avoid seeing the effect she had on him. She cocked one eyebrow, half in amusement and half in intense curiosity. A strange smile of satisfaction curled the corner of her mouth. "A gentleman through and through. Follow me." Her fingers entwined with his, leaving him no choice but to go with.

These were the only times he ever entered a woman's

bedchamber without there being a gravely ill occupant in the bed, and a witness for propriety. The room was as equally as feminine as the parlour, with pinks and mauves softening the furnishing and curtains. She closed the door with a quiet click, and led him to the edge of the purple, silk bedcover.

"Sit," she instructed quietly. He did, and she lowered herself onto his lap, tensing as the boldness of his groin betrayed him. She wriggled further onto his lap. By the holy waters of Babylon, he was about to faint with the exquisitely painful ecstasy of it. He curled his hands around her waist, pulling her closer. Was this what she desired? She draped her arms about his neck, kissing his face, his eyes, his ears, his neck with the lightest touches that left moist tingles on his skin. Her mouth completely covered his—the silkiness of her tongue always caught him by surprise. And what her tongue and teeth were doing to his lip right now almost stopped his heart! When she finally drew back, Billy was amused to find his shirt and buttons undone. A consummate professional, indeed!

"Loosen my hair," she whispered.

He enjoyed this the most about her—her explicit instructions that he was only too happy to obey. With trembling fingers, he withdrew the combs, and her thick locks poured over her shoulders like molten chocolate lava flecked with reds and golds. He grabbed a fistful, inhaling deeply and closing his eyes in pleasure. The sweet woody scent of cloves mingling with orange blossom jolted his senses more violently than smelling salts.

She wound a trail of soft hair around his nape like a scarf, and he shivered. She smiled. "Like my hair, do you?"

He wanted to grab two fistfuls of it and pull her in for another one of those delicious kisses, but instead gave an affirmative choking noise. "What would *you* like?" he asked, instantly scrunching his eyes in regret. Her hands framed his face, and he opened one eye. She was looking at him quite peculiarly. He opened his other eye to return her stare.

Her gaze was so direct his vision dipped. He had seen plenty of undressed bodies in his lifetime—male and female. The human body was functional and quite effective in many regards, and he rarely viewed it with anything but a professional eye. Mrs Teller rose, her dress puddling at her feet, rendering her as bare as the day she was born. Sweet Mary mother!

"You're—beautiful!"

She laughed lightly. "Get away. You've seen me plenty a time in the flesh."

"In my occupation, one does not usually get to admire a body so pink and healthy, and—well—*alive*!"

His breath quickened as she slid her hands over the scenic curve of her hips and down her thighs. His eyes caught a guilty glance at her most private and intimate of—*oh, God*! She stepped forward. He was fit to explode in an instant. Focusing on something, *anything*, else to prevent this impending calamity, he deeply wished for her to kiss him again. "What would you like me to do?" he asked, his confidence strengthening.

She leaned over, and drew his chin up, her hot breath in his ear whispering *precisely* what it was she wanted.

Billy reared back, a gasp bursting from him. "You wish me to perform manual pelvic massage, as I would to treat hysteria?"

"In a fashion." Mrs Teller smiled knowingly, running a soft-tipped finger across his lips. "Except I'd like you to use your tongue."

<hr />

SEAGULL CRIES FLOATED in on the breeze cooling the sweat on Billy's bare skin. He wound one of Mrs Teller's auburn tendrils around his long index finger, appreciating the silky slide of it across his skin. Her head rested on his thundering chest, her arm draped casually across his bare midriff, seemingly content to lay in his arms in the heaving aftermath, her own rapid breathing slowing.

Nothing on earth was as pleasurable as what she showed him time and time again. He was tempted to tip her onto her back and kiss her deeply. What other way was there to convey how much he loved her just at this minute? What a ludicrous notion for a man in his position. Still, one could not help what the heart wanted.

He spoke shyly, "Should you require more salves and bandages, I'd be only too happy to deliver them again. And, of course, your laudanum."

"I appreciate that, Dr Sykes." She traced the dark trail of hair on his stomach.

"Might I be so bold as to ask who the salve is for?" Billy asked.

She snorted derisively. "That bastard, Banks, might be government administrator, but he's no gentleman. He made a right mess of my Bessie."

Billy pursed his lips. "Do you wish me to examine her?"

Mrs Teller shook her head. "No. You know my girls take care of one another well enough." He tensed at her dismissal, but she drew little circles with her forefinger around his naval by way of appeasement, and his abdomen clenched. "But you can examine me again if you like?"

Billy propped himself on one elbow, his jaw tightened with seriousness. "I really *would* like to examine you." He slid his voice into a professional tone, and lay a hand on her conveniently bare midriff. His fingers palpated the spot on her stomach she had gripped earlier.

She giggled, and swatted his chest. "That tickles."

"Lay still," he murmured, his fingers working around the softness of her belly, feeling her liver. "How have you been feeling? Any nausea? Loss of appetite? Any changes to your waters?"

"My waters?" her tone piqued in surprise. "A word of advice, Doctor." She offered an indulgent smile. "You might wish to refrain from referring to a woman's bodily functions in the aftermath of pleasuring her. It rather takes the shine off the moment."

Billy stared, unblinking. "*How* have you been feeling?" he repeated firmly. He eased her eyelid down with his thumb. Was that a touch of jaundice in the sclera?

"Oh, very well, grumpy," she sighed, swatting his hand away. "Been a bit tired lately, and off my food, but 'tis the pain in my side that's the worst. It comes and goes. Nothing your laudanum can't help. If it's too tender, I nurse a bit of Angel's Kiss from Wang Mo Chou, from his den at the docks. You know the one? Beside Melva Dodson's gin house? Of course, as a woman, I can't head down into the basement where the den is—men's business only—but I have my runners."

Billy made a noise of derision through his nose. He knew all too well about the opium sold by the Chinaman. It was a great pain reliever for those suffering genuine afflictions, but the lure of the Devil's Smoke was a curse to those addicted to it.

"Opium is not to be trifled with," he warned. "It's dangerous when put to ill use."

"How can there be danger when it unclutters my mind, and gives me such clarity of thought? Gin and the like clouds my brain and trips my tongue, but just a few puffs of my Angel's Kiss is enough to sharpen my wit against any educated gentleman who walks through my doors."

"The stuff is a vice, petal. I've seen first-hand the damage it can do. Cravings that drive a person to unimaginable depravity for just one more puff. Pinpricked eyes of a mind lost in senselessness. Skin torn from the arms by the inescapable itch. Unless you require it to alleviate serious pain, I urge you to use it sparingly. Or avoid it altogether if you can."

Mrs Teller's fingers spread out like a starfish on his chest as she pushed him back down onto the pillow. She folded her hands on his pectoral muscle and rested her chin on them, smiling fondly. "I can take care of me and my own, Doctor. Never needed a man to take care of me before. No need for you to be galloping in on your white steed now."

Carbuncled boils, her flippancy stung—a lot! Not wanting her to move away from him just yet, he pressed his lips together and said nothing.

Mrs Teller settled her head on his chest again, releasing a long sigh. "Granted, my girls have a better life than most, but for some fellers, it doesn't matter whether they're paying five shillings or five pounds, they think they can make do as they please. There are establishments around for that sort of *entertainment*. Mine isn't one of them."

Billy wanted to smile, to run his hand down her slim back and to cup her buttocks appreciatively, but instead he curled his hands into fists, a cold eel of hurt squirming inside his belly. This is all he was to her. Entertainment.

At his silence, Mrs Teller's golden gaze snapped up sharply, her red lips parting as she laughed. "What did you think this was, doctor? I'm a whore. Not a cheap one, mind you, but a whore nonetheless. Mark me, you'll be back. Needs must."

"I had no intention of sampling your wares today before you stuck your tongue down my throat," quipped Billy, jamming his hands behind his head to stop them wandering over her soft, warm skin.

Mrs Teller laughed again, and this time it felt like she *was* mocking him. "You may be an educated man, but you're still a man. You all have the same needs. Rather it be me you give your run goods to than some poxy dock whore."

"Very well. I shall fetch your coin," he said stiffly, wriggling from under her.

She gripped his hip, halting his slide off the bed. "Don't tell me you're soft on me, you silly bastard?"

Billy's ears burned.

She made a gentle noise of contrition in her throat. "Don't worry, my lovely, today is on the house. In fact, I'm rather ravenous for a second helping." Elongating her neck, she kissed his lips again.

Billy almost groaned aloud as her tongue probed for his. The witch had a spell over him, and he was powerless to resist. "I can't," he gasped, snapping his head aside.

"My, my. You're a man of firsts, Dr Sykes. Never had a man say no to me before." She looked amused.

"Sorry, petal. I must go."

"But I want to apologise for my harsh words." Mrs Teller's full bottom lip jutted out playfully as her hand slid down his belly. "I don't mind if it's quick," she toyed, her fingers working expertly.

Despite everything, he groaned and squirmed. Wrestling his weakening willpower, Billy rolled away from the temptation, and swung his legs over the mattress edge. "No, I can't. I promised my assistant I'd be back after lunch. We've a sizeable order to fulfil for Gilly Downs."

"Fine specimen like you must be lonely living above a potions shop." The minx was not about to make it easy for him, and she raked one nail gently down the length of his back. "'Tis not every day I invite a man to stay in my bed without payment. Are you telling me I've lost my touch?"

Billy shivered and glanced over his shoulder. Her eyes were heavy with pleasure. Nothing could *possibly* come of this union. The sooner he accepted the limitations of their arrangement, the easier it would become. He shook his head. "No." He chuckled at her audaciousness. "You've a spell-binding touch that pins a man against his will." He caressed a finger along her refined jawline.

"Perhaps I *am* a witch?" She peered surreptitiously from beneath her long eyelashes, her fingers idly twirling the dark hairs on his thigh.

"Were that true, then perhaps you'd have a potion to cure my previous patient?" He felt his smile slip a little.

Mrs Teller's mouth pursed, and she arched one eyebrow. "What's it that ails the poor soul?"

Billy rubbed his face. "'Tis bearing children that's killing her. You women are all born for it, so I can't fathom how some manage with ease while it destroys others."

Mrs Teller sat up and, in all her naked splendour, swung her legs out of bed, gnawing her bottom lip in contemplation. "Ever heard of peacock flower?" Her voice was low and secretive.

Billy studied her a moment, then shook his head. "Can't say I have. Do you know the species name—its scientific name?"

"No, sorry."

"Why do you mention it?" His natural curiosity at the mention of a new plant piqued.

Mrs Teller picked up his hand and, turning it over, traced the lines on his palm with her thumb. "Ever wondered how it is we madams keep our girls in good health and without child?"

"I assumed you have your methods." Billy shrugged. "Ways in which we mere men are not privy to, and ones the church is disinclined to support."

The madam regarded him closely, her beautiful face tight with consideration. Was she measuring him for a deeper level of trust? His heart flipped. Thistles and dill, she was a whore—not some prospective bride! Though he could not help feeling an odd lightness in his chest when he saw her reach a decision.

"You know Alpharita, my beauty from the West Indies?"

"I do," said Billy, picturing the long-lashed woman he had seen in the public parlour downstairs.

"She's in great demand with the officialdom of Sydney Town who, bored with their pudgy dumplings at home, come here for the promise of a little spice. When Alpharita came to me three years ago, she brought a purse full of seeds. Asked if she could plant them out front, promising me a garden full of beautiful blooming shrubs."

Billy inclined his head and hummed. "I've noticed them. They certainly have just as alluring a charm as their mistress." He bravely leaned towards her, his heart skipping a beat as she tipped her chin up for a kiss. She smiled demurely against his lips at his compliment. Pulling back, Billy asked, "Are *they* the mysterious peacock flower to which you refer?"

She nodded. "A decoction of the root serves as a menstrual stimulator. It remedies even the *gravest* of female problems." Mrs Teller held her breath as she measured his reaction.

Interested, Billy narrowed his eyes, bringing the physician and apothecary in him to the fore. Here was the promise of a solution to a problem for which he had no fix. And certainly, in the case of Erin Hicks, anything that could prevent her from conceiving another child would most certainly lessen the risk on her life. "What of its toxicity? Its side effects?" he asked with professional stoicism, his own naked proximity to this enchanting creature almost forgotten.

Mrs Teller gave him a pained look of ignorance, gentled by a reluctant smile. "I've no information on the plant other than to tell you that it *works*. I've personally experienced nothing more than an occasional headache or an upset stomach. Short-term inconveniences that far outweigh the long-term benefits."

"In what quantity?" His professional candour overrode any emotional or moral dilemmas, his mind honed on the scientific and biological possibilities of this new treatment.

"One cup of decoction twice a day does the trick," she said pragmatically.

Billy pulled his hand back from her, and stood up to retrieve his hastily discarded clothes. "Fascinating," he muttered, his mind whirling with the possibilities. "Utterly fascinating." He dressed mindlessly, lost in a myriad of thoughts. Just imagine the help he could offer the poor wretches in The Rocks' slums. Their endlessly churning out children left them poorer and hungrier with every additional mouth to feed. He spun to look at her again, tucking his shirt-tails into his trousers. "And there are truly no dire side effects?"

Mrs Teller stretched out on the bed, her spectacularly naked body wholly unmarked by the ravages of any pregnancy. "Do I look like damaged goods to you?"

Billy stepped forward and ventured to cup a heavy breast in his hand. Thrilled that she did not resist, he pressed her into the soft mattress with a deep kiss. "No, you don't, petal," he said, smiling as she laughed and raked her fingers through his hair. The excitement built in him again like a fierce electric storm brewing on the horizon. With an effort, he drew back, sitting heavily on the bed to pull on his shoes. "Do you have a decoction at hand?" he asked, looking hopefully at her.

"I do," said Mrs Teller, sliding off the bed, and slipping into a lavender silk gown smattered with small yellow flowers. "The seeds grow in pods, not unlike peas. I've a sizeable seed collection if you wish to propagate your own plants?"

Billy cocked his head. "Alas, living above the apothecary has its advantages, but the pleasure of a garden isn't one. Do you perhaps have roots to spare?"

She paused, studying him with one eye closed. "I do. But it'll cost you."

The cold reality of the situation slid down his nape like a trickle of rainwater under his collar. He firmed his face into a businesslike fashion. "Of course, Mrs Teller. How much?" Regretting not maintaining a professional distance, he did not use an endearment.

Mrs Teller laughed lightly, and he frowned, unsure whether she was laughing at him again. With a provocative sashaying of her hips, she approached, the gown's silk belt untying, and showing a delicate peep of skin, naval, and dark curls. *Control yourself man!* He ground his teeth in self-recrimination as he felt himself stir again. She stepped up close to him, hovering, not touching. Billy swallowed deeply. This was worse than if she lay her hands on him.

She cast her brilliant blue gaze up. "Why Dr Sykes, I'm not after your money." Her soft purr ignited his blood.

"You're not?" He took a small step back in surprise. "More laudanum then?"

"Why, no. I simply ask for your escort to the races at Home-bush next weekend." She offered a disarming smile. "Being draped on the arm of a respectable doctor such as yourself will do wonders for my—constitution."

Not to mention what it would do to his reputation!

"Mrs Teller, the honour would be mine," he said, bowing deeply. "However, I've been invited to Gilly Downs, out west, for Christmas. I depart the day after tomorrow."

She tutted playfully. "What a pity. I was so looking forward to having you unwrap me again on Christmas Day."

Chapter Four

ADELIA SHYLING

BARCLAY HALL, NEW SOUTH WALES, 16 DECEMBER 1853

1 PM.

Surrounded by the sultry afternoon air, Adelia traced a finger around the white-painted wrought-iron whorls of the outdoor table. Barclay Hall's wide wrap-around veranda caught the cool breeze blowing up from the creek below. She sipped another taste of Cook's newly brewed ginger beer, wincing at the bite in her throat and burn through her nose. "A bit astringent for my liking. It's spoiling the taste of Cook's roast lamb."

Mr Shyling dug between his teeth with the nail on his little finger, kept longer than the rest for this purpose, and sucked the dislodged food free. "While it's a great charm of life to be drunk, this poison isn't the way to it." He flicked his glass, showering the purple bougainvillea flowers with a splash. Her giant, dark-haired husband grinned, softening his masculine features.

"Mr Shyling!" Adelia flicked a glance around to see if Cook was about. She shook her head and chuckled. "Let Cook hear you say that and it'll be doughy damper for you for the next month." She relished these luncheons with her husband. With so many chores pulling them apart from dawn until dusk, this midday meeting provided a brief one-hour sanctuary they both looked forward to. It was a habit born from the days when the children ate luncheon in the children's dining room, leaving Adelia the rare luxury of time alone with her new husband. A new husband who her first husband, Mr Barclay, had planted in his stead. Lying in a rain-soaked pasture with his neck broken from a falling branch, Elijah Barclay had implored Victor Shyling to take care of her and the children. This quiet, New Zealand pastoralist, whose own life mirrored Adelia's with the loss of his wife and two step-daughters, had taken his vow to a dying man to heart. When Mr Shyling's duties kept him around the homestead, he never missed a single midday meal with her.

Mr Shyling continued detailing the new wool-screw-press's intricacies, and she leaned forward, attentively, her interest in the machinery matching her husband's. Under his excellent steward-ship, Gilly Downs had expanded over the years.

"It's all very well to add new machinery, but is there the labour to man it?" she asked.

Mr Shyling sucked in a deep breath that expanded his barrelled chest. "With so many shearers chancing their fate on the goldfields, we'll be lucky to find enough men to fill all eighty stalls. Even the shepherds will have to turn their hand to shearing. This season's clip will be a family affair. Noah's old enough and strong enough to help me bale. The two youngest can tar wounds."

"Last season, Ruthie developed quite an eye for classing the wool with me. She can help me again, even though she'll no doubt have a grumble about it. She'd prefer helping Cook pick seeds from the raisins."

"Classing might not be as pleasant as food preparation, but it yields more money." He ran a thick, muscly hand down his whiskers and locked his gaze onto her. "Have I told you what a wonder you are, Mrs Shyling?"

The warmth of his flattery surged up her torso and burst across her cheeks. "Once or twice." She giggled.

When she looked back on their marriage, it struck her that the wedding itself was the moment when their relationship had shifted. She had handed him her trust. Given him her business, her family, herself—put them all into his keeping. And he had not failed her.

The place of understanding, of pure pleasure, she had found with him on their wedding night had not faded over the years either. He had the muscle and size to dominate, yet the perfume of their mingled bodies moving together, despite the swell of her advanced state, was nothing she had ever experienced before. The robust and intoxicating smell of him afterwards had left her wanting more. She had never told anyone, not even Grace Fitzwilliam, but she swore it was his attentive ministrations the following night that brought little Moses Elijah's arrival on three weeks early.

"Has Clodagh returned to her duties?" he asked, lowering his voice a notch.

Clodagh, the Irish nursey maid, travelled to the colony with her friend Afric, back when Elijah was still alive. Despite a hasty wedding to the Italian shepherd Roberto Rossi resulting in a bouncing boy arriving a couple of months early, Afric, now respectably married, had been promoted to housekeeper. Clodagh was another matter altogether.

Adelia snorted. "She has, the little trollop. I hope she's

learned her lesson. There'll be no more liberties in allowing her to leave the property on her days off."

"Rightly so," nodded Mr Shyling. "'Tis only by God's good grace the jury saw sense to reimburse me some of my expenses."

As Clodagh's employer, Mr Shyling sued assistant colonial surgeon John Silverman for seducing the girl. Adelia folded her arms. "Twenty-five pounds barely made up for losing the girl's services during her dalliance. Poor Afric was left to manage the household *and* the children."

"Perhaps my claim for two hundred pounds was a little optimistic?" Mr Shyling's broad, red nose scrunched. "Pity the broadsheets caught wind of it. Then again, the girl played with fire and got burnt."

What the broadsheets neglected to report was that that soon after the trial, Dr Silverman's wife arrived from England and became a fixture at her husband's side, leaving the silly girl destitute and alone, or that Mr Shyling had personally fetched her from town.

"She's lucky she's kept her position and hasn't been demoted to scullery maid," said Adelia sharply.

"Were her services about the homestead not in such high demand, I'd have sent her out to serve as Hicks and Wilkinson's hut-keeper." Mr Shyling rasped a square-nailed thumb through his black whiskers, his thick, strong fingers curling. "She'd know all about hard work then, scratching the dirt to grow vegetables, and hauling those hurdles to move the sheep yards around. She'd have had her fair share of watching the yarded flocks at night, not to mention keeping the shepherds fed and watered."

Adelia hummed in agreement. "Might be worth considering sending her out there with Opal McDermott? They could serve as one another's chaperone, or ultimately both end up shepherd's wives! Though, the children were eager to have her back home. Ruthie pleaded her case most pitifully."

Mr Shyling chortled. "That maid could herd cats and get

them to toe the line. God knows, no one on earth kept our rabble under control like she did when they were younger."

Adelia tipped her head back and laughed. "Too true, my dear! Too true."

"How is the new governess faring?" Mr Shyling slapped at a mosquito on his broad wrist with lethal agility that belied his size. He was seated two arm-lengths from her, solid like a stone lion, and she absorbed the promise of protection that glinted in his brown eyes. His broad frame commanded respect from other men who recognised where the power lay, and obeyed it. He leaned forward and slid his hand over hers, his calloused touch as gentle as a kitten's paw.

"Miss Steele is living up to her name, with an iron will not easily swayed by the foibles of mischievous children. She's not easily scared by toads in her desk drawer, or deterred by Moses bringing her a dead snake to dissect."

"How very game of her." His deep-throated chuckle matched the amusement in his dark eyes.

The children had been at Madame Dubois' boarding school in town for their younger years. Even after Miss Lissing became Mrs Toby Hicks, she had continued to teach, but she had recently stepped away from the classroom again to await another confinement. As soon as each Barclay child turned ten, Mr Shyling broached the merits of having them at the station to help with the chores about the homestead, and up at the shed too. Unable to fault his reasoning, Adelia had negotiated with him to hire a governess, allowing the children to continue their lessons while still helping about the property.

Her own business acumen had been born of a generous father who, accepting his lot of having four daughters, was determined to make them useful sources of information in the marriages he arranged. Having daughters able to interpret a balance sheet and disseminate the fine print in a contract had come in handy for his investments over the years. Not that she reported anything to him these days, since he had long passed away. Gilly Downs was hers and Mr Shyling's alone.

Noah at sixteen, Gideon at thirteen, and Moses at eleven were old enough to climb into the wood loft, throw down the wood, carry it down to blacksmith, in the smithing shed. Once Nevin Buchanan's job, Gideon and Moses were now responsible for daily digging, picking and plucking fresh vegetables.

Ruth at fifteen and Eve at fourteen proved practical in the kitchen. With the shearing shed's expansion resulting in so many more mouths to feed, Cook needed help greasing tins for damper and scones. This became the girls' daily chore. Their nimble hands also made light of shelling peanuts and spreading them on trays, ready for Cook to roast. Of course, the perk of working in the kitchen was being allowed a taste of whatever treat Cook was whipping up. Treacle pudding, which she needed Ruthie's de-seeded raisins for, was a real treat. Adelia was secretly impressed watching her girls manage to keep the fire banked *and* keep the pot on a rolling boil to prevent the pudding from getting heavy. Cooking was certainly not her forte.

Mr Shyling's thick brows dipped as he stared into the distance towards the stables, where Noah was tasked with caring for the impressive number of horses now stabled at Gilly Downs. Twisting, Adelia glanced over her shoulder.

"Moses!" She burst from her seat, and the iron chair's clawed-feet gouged the veranda deck.

Noah sprinted jerkily down the hill like a disoriented scarecrow, his efforts hampered by the floppy-limbed body of his little brother in his arms. "Mama! Papa!" Noah's baritone voice cracked into a high squeak.

Moses's shrill shrieks echoing up the valley were swallowed by the thundering rush of blood in Adelia's ears. The unsweetened ginger beer on her tongue soured to the bitter bile of fear. Behind her, Mr Shyling grunted, and his heavy boots thundered down the painted steps onto the gravel carriage circle. He met

Noah at the lawn's edge and scooped Moses from his arms. Their son looked so tiny crushed against her husband's broad chest.

She sucked in a breath. "What happened?"

Blood dribbled from the lower half of Moses's freckled face, still plump with childhood, and he opened a bloodied hand. His dirt-encrusted palm nestled three white teeth like pearls in a clamshell. "Mma—" A gloopy bubble of snot and blood popped on his lips as he mumbled her name.

"Coming through!" Mr Shyling thundered through the front door.

Running behind her husband, Adelia snatched Noah's arm, her fingers barely able to curl around his thick bicep. He smelled of crushed leaves and leather, the gamy undertone of aging saddles marred by the sharp stink of fear. "Noah! What happened to your brother?"

Her eldest son's red cheeks matched his flaming hair, his blue eyes saucers of panic. "Lantern kicked him."

"What on earth were you doing letting him near her." She pounded up the sweeping staircase behind Mr Shyling, sidestepping the drips of blood on the plush, patterned stair runner.

Noah scraped his fingers through his ruddy thatch before gripping a handful. "She's the gentlest of all our mares. I never thought she'd—"

She shook Noah's arm, her voice pitching. "She's *just* foaled for the first time. You should never have let him—"

"I know, Mama. He wanted to give her a carrot. I told him not to enter her stall, but he didn't listen."

She unclutched his arm and burst into Moses's bedchamber, scrambling to his side as Mr Shyling deposited him onto the cover as though he were made of glass. Moses looked up at her, his blue eyes bloodshot and puffy from crying. He opened his palm again and wailed at the three teeth. Adelia scooped away the bloodied evidence and tucked them behind the lantern on the side table.

"I'm here, angel pie. All will be well."

Noah danced from one foot to the other. "Shall I fetch Wee Granny Mac? I'll put her in the wheelbarrow if I have to."

"Let the old woman be," said Mr Shyling calmly. The mattress sank and the bedframe creaked as he lowered himself beside the small boy. Taking out his clean, folded handkerchief, he gently wadded it between Moses's bleeding lips. He tenderly stroked the hair back from Moses's brow, his voice lightly chiding, "You great big dafty. You won't ever approach a new foal again, will you?"

Moses made a strangled noise as he attempted to shake his head, his little face crumpling in a world of pain as he clutched the side of his head. The white handkerchief bloomed red.

Mr Shyling met Adelia's gaze, his lips disappearing into his thick, black whiskers as he hummed. "Broken jaw?"

Oh, God above, let it not be so! Adelia placed her hand on Moses's chest, his thumping heart against her palm like that of a chick chased by a rooster. She glowered at Noah. "Fetch a jug of clean water."

"Yes, Mama." Noah bounced from the room.

Mr Shyling gestured towards the hiding teeth. Those are his adult teeth. If I don't try re-seat them, he'll be toothless for life."

Adelia frowned at the three blood-stumped teeth. He was right, of course, but the thought of inflicting further pain on her youngest child sent a shiver across her nape.

"Just a minute." She eased herself off the mattress, and scurried to the main bedchamber. She hauled out the medicinal box from the bottom of her wardrobe. Sliding it onto the foot of Moses's bed, she unlatched the lid and peered in at the neat, velvet-lined compartments where everything had its place. She picked up the clear laudanum bottle, it's half full contents sloshing she turned it over to read the dosage label. *Five years old, 25 drops. Adults, 1 teaspoonful.* Moses was ten. So, perhaps thirty drops? No, forty. She wanted him asleep. It was the last bottle, but Dr Sykes would replenish her stock in a few days. If only he were here already!

After a while, Moses's eyes rolled like they had when he was a babe fighting off sleep in her arms. She stroked a soothing finger down his forehead, encouraging his eyes to close and stay shut. He let out the deep double sigh that had always been the signal of his slide into slumber since he was tiny. She nodded at her husband.

Mr Shyling pushed the teeth firmly back into the bruised and swollen gums with a slow, steady pressure, the corded muscles of his forearms flexing at the delicate job. His bearded face twitched in concentration. Adelia wanted to turn from the sickening squelches that she felt all the way down to her soul, but she pried Moses's lips apart while her husband held the teeth in place a while longer.

She stitched her son's split top lip with a painstakingly neat row of stitches garnered from years of needlework, glad her son was not awake to feel the gut pulling the wound's flaps together. Her imagination toyed with her—was that moan at the back of his throat? She ran her tongue over her own lip. Her skin, tingling in sympathy, tasted sweet and clean, and not salty or on fire as Moses's would be when he awoke. Done with the gruesome task, she leaned back to admire the coarse, stiff stitches in the purple, swollen flesh.

Mr Shyling harrumphed and nodded. "I doubt even Dr Sykes could have done a better job."

He carefully strapped Moses's jaw in a full-headed sling that wrapped under his chin and tied atop his head. He had devised the contraption from a thick piece of tent canvas that he lined with muslin to prevent the youngster's cheeks from chaffing. He fastened the laces over Moses's red curls.

"When he awakens, he can let us know if he needs it tightening or loosening for comfort," he explained. "The sling should remove most of his pain when walking and sleeping." He patted

Moses's head gently. "Now, he must get on with the job of heal-
ing." His words, while pragmatic, were not unkindly spoken.

"How long before we know whether the teeth have taken
root?"

Her husband's broad shoulders hunched up to his handsome,
hairy jowls. "'Tis anyone's guess."

"He'll be on liquids for months, won't he?" She stroked the
youthful chubbiness of his brow. It would not stay plump for
much longer.

"He will," concurred Mr Shyling, rising from the bed.

Adelia rounded her shoulders. "He was so looking forward to
Christmas dinner with everyone. You know how much he enjoys
his food."

"I'm sure Cook will relish putting her experimental culinary
skills to good use to keep the lad nourished over the next little
while. Let's just keep that god-awful ginger swill away from
him." The floorboards creaked as he stepped over and drew her
into his arms, holding her tight. "Come here, sweetheart. All will
be well."

Her thighs were weak and watery, and she wanted to plop to
the floor, but he gripped her tightly. She knew he would not drop
her. Over the years, the weight of their new life together, the
responsibilities of Gilly Downs and the children, distributed
itself from her shoulders onto his, and he shared the weight with
the sincerest sense of duty. He bore the burden equally in a way
that never diminished her authority. Their union created harmony
within her family, and the perfect balance at Gilly Downs. But at
times like this, she was glad to feel him quietly pull a little more
of the worry from her while she regained her strength.

She needed all her wits about her for the Christmas Day
gathering. There were still gumnut wreaths to be hung in the
windows, veranda railings to festoon with greenery, and candles
to make. Mr Singh, the trader, had tried to coerce Cook into
buying some prohibitively expensive candles made from

cinnamon and yak butter, imported from his home country, India. An eternal pinchpenny, Cook had shooed him away and attempted her own rendition from cinnamon bark and beeswax, guaranteeing their heady scent would bring a festive cheer to the upcoming Christmas festivities. Adelia remembered back to her arrival at Gilly Downs as a new bride, and the horror of her first lesson of preparing slush lamps from rendered mutton fat. Cook had not ceased forcing her to broaden her homemaker skills over the years. Of all the stars above, hopefully the woman's Christmas candles would be more successful than her ginger beer!

A chorus of laughter from outside grew louder, accompanied by the tramp of footsteps across the veranda. Ruthie's excitable laugh burst up the stairs, then faded to a murmur as the group moved into the dining room below.

"Sounds like they're back." Mr Shyling's deep voice resonated from deep inside his chest, the rumble comforting against her cheek. Clodagh, Emily and Eve had been out gathering foliage for the decorations.

Reluctantly releasing his solid waist, Adelia stepped back and scraped loose strands of hair from her face. She turned on her brightest smile. "Right, those table centrepieces aren't going to make themselves. Clodagh can sit with Moses. The girls and I will spend this afternoon weaving wreaths. Now, where did I put that red ribbon?"

Chapter Five

EMILY FITZWILLIAM

PITT STREET, SYDNEY TOWN, 16 DECEMBER 1853

5.30 PM.

The bell above Mrs Moore's dress shop door tinkled as it shut after the bustling last-minute shopper. Emily bounded over to Mamam on the footpath, and looped arms with her, drawing her in from the sea of other shop employees and factory workers who had all clocked-off and were hastily retreating home. She tugged Mamam another step forward, hoping she might strike up a conversation with Mrs Moore. Of course, it was also the perfect excuse to fill her senses with the sight and voice of Mrs Moore's handsome son a moment longer.

Mrs Moore turned the brass key in the lock with a loud snap, and slid it into the tapestried reticule purse dangling from her wrist. Her hair was drawn back so tightly under her black felt hat that it drew her eyes into slants beneath the low-pulled brim. Emily always thought she looked petite and elegant enough to be a ballerina. Beneath that hat, her once inky hair was now streaked equally with white. She must have had her son at a rather mature age since her face was more lined than Mamam's or Cappy's.

"Good afternoon, Mrs Moore. Mr Moore." Mamam greeted.

A discrete soft cough turned all three women towards the tall man's bowed head, his feet shuffling at suddenly finding their eyes upon him. Mr Moore bowed at Mamam, dipping his head and giving a warm, full-lipped smile that opposed his mother's stony countenance. "Good afternoon, madam."

"Mrs Fitzwilliam," said Mrs Moore, her deep, throaty hum that of a smoker. Taking her son's offered elbow, she peered from beneath the brim of her hat.

Mr Moore's dark eyes flashed across to Emily, his calculated smile revealing a row of white, slightly crooked bottom teeth, which did nothing to detract her from his charm. A charm that attracted her, not to the rich dark brown of his eyes that matched his hair, but to the adoration on his face whenever he spoke to his mother. Oh, that she might earn some of that devotion for herself!

Emily smiled shyly before averting her eyes to the safe territory of Mamam's face. Seeing Mr Moore's smile widen into an interested grin from the corner of her eye, Emily was unable to stop her mouth from tweaking up in a smile.

Mrs Moore's raspy voice broke the silence. "Off somewhere special with your daughter, Mrs Fitzwilliam?"

"To sup at the Australian Hotel. And you?"

"Joseph and I are on our way home, aren't we, pet?"

"Would you care to join us?" blurted Emily. Her scalp ignited as all three faces turned sharply towards her. Good gracious, could Mr Moore feel the heat radiating off her?

Mr Moore's eyes transformed from wide orbs of surprise to lash-lowered slits of delight. He turned to his mother, one brow raised, respectfully awaiting her reply.

"Oh, no. We couldn't possibly." Mrs Moore shook her head. "It would be rude of us to impose without proper notice."

Emily squeezed Mamam's arm. She had never been the type of child to ask for things in Edwin's repetitive manner, which either led Mamam to capitulate to keep the nagging at bay, or forced Cappy to use his captain's voice to quell the domestic mutiny. Instead, she had perfected an innocent look of expectation that turned Cappy into a mush of porridge, and charmed Mamam into consent. She used it sparingly enough that it was rare for either parent to deny her.

Smiling magnanimously, Mamam returned the squeeze, and whipped her face to Mrs Moore. "It's no imposition at all. I insist. Please do join us."

Mrs Moore bristled primly. "Very well."

With Mrs Moore and her son following behind, Emily pressed Mamam along the uneven pavement, keeping clear of the emerging night workers whose trades were so noxious they could only be carried out under the discreet cover of evening.

Mamam put a protective arm across Emily to stop her from crossing the street as a dunny man plodded past with his night-soil cart. Emily pressed a finger beneath her nose as the vaporous odour of human excrement that followed the unfortunate fellow reached her. Not put out by her reaction, the grizzled grey-whiskered man gave her a slow smile, and touched the brim of his hat with one grimy-nailed finger. With manners borne by instinct, she dropped her hand, returning his greeting with a smile and a dip of her head. Darting between the clatter of an oncoming hackney carriage and the rumbling cart of a rat catcher piled with his empty wire cages and tin buckets, Mamam hurried her to the opposite pavement.

"Wouldn't want to be wandering this part of town after dark," grumbled Mrs Moore from behind.

"There's been a widespread plea to the governor for gas lighting to be installed," placated Mr Moore.

Mrs Moore's graceful hand arched through the air. "Do you see any lighting?" she said starchily.

"Lighting certainly serves a purpose to discourage lawless gangs of scoundrels hanging about," said Mamam over her shoulder.

Emily glanced back too. "They'll no doubt find other parts of town where the night's anonymity offers them sanctuary."

Mrs Moore raised her nose. "I care not where they choose to loiter as long as it's *not* near me."

"Fear not, Mother. We're here now." Mr Moore held open the door of the Australian Hotel, its lantern light within twinkling in welcome.

They were shown to a cosy table tucked in the corner. Mr Moore pulled out his mother and Emily's chairs simultaneously. Emily lowered herself to his right, and glanced around the hotel dining room. While not the silver service Cappy spoke of in London, the restaurant was pleasantly decorated, and was clearly one of the fancier establishments in this town of taverns. The murmur of conversation and occasional clink of silverware against china was a world away from the raucous din of tin spoons scraping wooden bowls in The Sailor's Homecoming. The wooden floor shone with polish instead of spilled ale.

Mrs Moore must have noticed this too. "What a pleasant atmosphere. Quite endearing to induce one to appetite, wouldn't you agree, pet?"

"I would, Mother. I'm quite famished," enunciated Mr Moore, handing her a menu. He did not have a particularly deep voice, but he sounded quite the gentleman when he spoke.

Emily licked her lips to clear her smug smile as Mr Moore tried, and failed, to show discretion as he studied her in return. Thankfully both matriarchs were distracted by the menu, which gave them a chance to intimately scrutinise one another.

He could not be more than a couple of years older than her. He had the same face as his mother, except for the square chin, and while not strikingly handsome, he had a genteel quality about him that appealed to her sense of order. His hands that held the menu were wide and square, not long-fingered like Cappy or Eddy. The nail-stumps, while bitten to the quick, were clearly not subject to manual labour, with ink stains the only offence. Mr Moore, like his mother, sat upright in the chair with excellent posture.

Mrs Moore lowered her menu, and Mr Moore's lips twitched as he flicked a guilty look at his own menu. His forefinger absently picked at his stunted thumbnail.

"Do you dine here often, Mrs Fitzwilliam?" asked Mrs Moore.

"Yes. Once every couple of weeks, Emily and I meet. My husband's shipping company is not far from here."

"The one at Semi-circular Quay?" Mr Moore's slim black eyebrows arched.

Emily shuffled on the supple, padded seat. "You know of it?"

"Indeed," said the dark-haired man, his thick thumb toying with the menu's papery edge. "The Elias Shipping Company brought over our last shipment of fabric from London."

"Oh." Emily's words failed her. She had worked at Mrs Moore's dress shop for four years, and he had barely paid any attention to her until recently. She had not imagined he knew who she was all along. Emily tightened her grip on the menu. Of course he barely noticed, silly! Until recently, she had rarely been allowed in the front shop unless they were swamped. And even then, all she was permitted to do was point customers to what they might be looking for, or offer a cup of tea while they awaited Mrs Moore.

"Are you familiar with dress fitting, Mr Moore?" queried Mamam.

"No, madam. I manage the administrative business from a small office above the shop. Invoices and orders and such. Mother takes care of the dress and costume designs below."

Mamam tilted her head. "Costumes?"

"Yes," interjected Emily, feeling left out of the conversation. "Mrs Moore also supplies the costumes to Mr Creswick at The Cove Theatre."

"How exciting." Mischievously encouraged by her blushing, Mamam continued, "Emily, you've been scribbling outrageous designs for as long as I can remember. Perhaps Mr Creswick might care to have a look them?"

Mr Moore, looking suitably impressed, asked, "Have you had opportunity to sketch many gowns yet, Miss Fitzwilliam?"

Emily bit back a burst of laughter. Did he not know what a hard task-master his mother was? In her first year with Mrs Moore, the closest she had come to a needle and thread was sweeping them off the floor. The following couple of years had been all about petticoats, stays and children's clothes. Only last month had she been permitted to embroider her first bodice. Until then, she had been relegated to hemming, and attaching cuffs and collars.

"After the shop has closed, I sketch my ideas in my notebook so that I won't forget." Emily took a sip of wine that Mamam had ordered. Placing her glass next to Mr Moore's with a tiny chink, she angled her chin towards him. "And what of you, sir? Have you any secret talents you keep hidden from the world?"

"Alas, no secrets," he smiled, the lantern light reflecting playfully in his deep brown eyes. "Though I should confess, I manage a step or two at Mother's dances."

"Come now, son! Don't be so modest," interrupted Mrs

Moore. "You are an excellent dancer. Far better than your father ever was." Her voice quavered on this last sentence, and Mr Moore slid his hand over hers.

Licking his lips, he explained, "My father passed away when I was ten. An accident."

"It was *no* accident," retorted Mrs Moore, her thin lips puckering.

"Mother, don't upset yourself," Mr Moore chided. He glanced at Emily with an apologetic look. "Father's accident happened shortly after he published a complaint in the *Sydney Monitor*. Mother believes his death to be an act of foul play, but there is no evidence."

Emily tightened her brow in sympathy. "What was his complaint?" She flinched as Mamam's foot pressed down on hers under the table. Too late.

"Father was a stonemason. He employed his own men, and sold his stone for a moderate profit, but was precluded from hiring the government stone carts and teams due to his rival's private monopoly of them. He wanted to alert the public of this clandestine behaviour since no government tenders had been advertised. It was a fraud on all other quarrymen who dealt in stone and earned a living by it. He fought for all stonemasons and builders to have an equal right to buy government stone and hire government teams." Mr Moore took a deep mouthful of wine.

Mrs Moore made a slight noise in her throat. "That big mouth of his always put him in hot water. He always had a penchant for speaking up against corruption, even back in England—*even* if it was the *government* doing the corrupting. It's what got us exiled here."

"What happened?" asked Emily, her gaze fixed on Mr Moore. "The accident, I mean."

"Emily," cautioned Mamam in a low tone.

Mr Moore smiled in reassurance. "I don't mind speaking of

it." He turned to Emily and licked his lips again. "Father was struck by a carriage crossing the street near King's Wharf—um —before Semi-circular Quay was built. The driver didn't stop, and the witnesses didn't recognise the carriage. It was ruled an unfortunate accident."

The lining of Emily's stomach contracted. She lowered her head and pressed her eyelids tight for a moment before offering Mr Moore a pained look of empathy. "I'm truly sorry to hear that. I lost a brother to a carriage accident too." She lowered her eyes to the candle flickering between them, her voice dropping, "Many years ago now." Grey flashes of memory flickered before her—the carriage wheel spokes— Elias on his face in the mucky gutter—Sally's crushing grip on her hand—Mamam's screams. She jolted as her memories threw a coloured image into her face like a bucket of icy water —Elias's blood-streaked face as Mamam tried to jiggle him awake in the carriage.

She glanced up as Mrs Moore inhaled sharply. "Oh, Mrs Fitzwilliam. I cannot *imagine* the pain of losing a child." Mrs Moore's gaze roved from Mamam to her son, and he squeezed her fingers. "Joseph is my only child. I couldn't *live* without him."

The bow-tied publican arrived, and the business of discussing the freshness of the boiled cod with parsley sauce provided a timely distraction from the heavy subject. With all orders placed, Mr Moore turned to Emily, and leaned in.

"Do *you* like dancing, Miss Fitzwilliam?"

Emily regarded him a moment, her heart flopping side-to-side in her chest like a puppy's tail. "I do. Though, the only dancing I've done has been with my father in our front parlour, or with a female dance partner during dancing lessons at school." She shrugged. "Unless you count being whirled around in a high-speed jig by enthusiastic shepherds at Gilly Downs as dancing?"

Mr Moore's mouth twitched. "Well, I suppose a jig is a dance."

Mrs Moore's pert eyebrows snapped together. Was it the jig she disapproved of or the mention of her dancing with farmhands?

Mamam interjected hastily. "We are well acquainted with the Shylings. They are family friends and business acquaintances. We often visit them. In fact, Emily and her brother spent a good deal of their childhoods at Gilly Downs. Mrs Shyling has put on many a dance for the district to celebrate the end of each shearing season, though she rarely needs an excuse being such a social butterfly. At any sheep station, female dance partners of any age are always in great demand. The shepherds—"

"She permits the *hired help* to attend social gatherings?" Mrs Moore's voice crisped over.

Mamam's lips tightened. "Many of the Gilly Downs men are either crew from my husband's ships or shepherds who sought passage with us. My family has long-standing acquaintances with these good folks, including being indebted to some of them for saving our lives."

Mrs Moore elongated her long, graceful neck, bringing herself to her full height, her indignation poorly disguised behind a watery smile. "That's quite a noble point-of-view, Mrs Fitzwilliam. Though I dare say that socialising with convicts must bring about its share of issues, not the least of what it does for one's reputation."

Mamam's green eyes iced over, and Emily bit her lower lip. Oh no, she had not seen any man, woman, or child win any argument with Mamam when she had this look.

"I made no mention of convicts." Mamam bit off the edges of her words. "The Gilly Downs men are all free, by birth or ticket-of-leave."

Mrs Moore huffed delicately through her nose. "Hmph!

Ticket-of-leave men are merely convicts—" she narrowed her eyes "—*with privileges.*"

Mamam held Mrs Moore's gaze firmly with her own. "My husband and I support the egalitarian nature of this colony. Surely any man prepared to bend his back to provide a better life for himself and his family deserves equal opportunity, regardless of past indiscretions? Don't we all harbour something in our past that we seek to keep buried?"

Mrs Moore's slim face was tight and pale, and her husky voice deepened. "I take umbrage to your implication that everyone has something to hide—as though we are all somehow *common criminals.*"

Emily squeezed her eyes shut, taking in a deep calming breath. She reached for Mamam's hand under the table, and offered Mrs Moore a neutral smile. "Please, let's not spoil our evening." She studied the restaurant, searching for an excuse to introduce a new topic of conversation. A woman at the table nearest the door was fanning herself. The weather! One could never go wrong with that.

"Hasn't it been awfully muggy today, Mr Moore?" she said, glancing away from the feuding mothers and locking eyes with Mr Moore. He stabbed a forkful of beef steak, and hummed in agreement as he pressed his lips around the metal prongs of his fork to suppress his smile. Beneath the table, Mamam wriggled her fingers free from her grip, and patted the back of her hand in a silent promise to hold her tongue. Thank goodness!

Mr Moore chewed judiciously in the silence that followed, and swallowing asked, "Have you ever been to one of Mother's dances, Miss Fitzwilliam?"

Emily widened her eyes at his audaciousness for ignoring her hint to change subjects. Did he enjoy goading his mother? While not quite as elegant as the governor's balls, Mrs Moore's dances provided the solidly middle-income element of Sydney Town's society an excuse to meet, socialise, gossip and most importantly, match-make.

"No she hasn't," snapped Mrs Moore. "First hands aren't permitted to attend without being accompanied by a partner approved by me. The nearest this girl has come to attending one is to clear the sewing room and decorate it." She glowered at her son. "And don't call it a *dance*. Makes it sound no better than those vulgar music halls that have begun springing up. You'll find no convicts, workmen, or loose women at *my* soirees."

Stumbling in the face of such scorn, Emily stammered, "I'm s-sure everyone looks spectacular in their gowns and waistco—" She stopped, pinned into silence by Mrs Moore's unimpressed glare. Not wishing to show fear, Emily lifted her chin.

Sniffing, Mamam scrunched her nose, and Emily was thankful she kept her promise and did not give Mrs Moore a full serving.

Mr Moore's lips twitched as she shifted uncomfortably in her seat. "Spectacular indeed, Miss Fitzwilliam. The benefit of being the host of such occasions is that one is never short of a dance partner." Mr Moore's voice carried a teasing note, but his look was one of gentle amusement. "Though I've never had the pleasure of inviting a partner of *my* choosing."

Emily's cheeks warmed. What was he saying? Would he dare ask her? Surely he must know it would be against his mother's wishes.

Mr Moore gave a knowing nod, attempting unsuccessfully to smother his chuckle behind his napkin. "Pudding anyone? I hear sago custard a calling."

Mamam lay her napkin across her empty plate, and pierced Emily with a look that she should do the same. "No, thank you," said Mamam, rising. "Emily and I have some packing to do."

Mr Moore rose, and Mrs Moore jerked her head towards Emily, her bloodless lips pursed. "Where are you off to? I've granted no leave?"

"Mrs Shyling has invited us to Gilly Downs for Christmas, Mrs Moore." Emily wished the centre of the earth would open up. A jagged, rocky, black hole surrounded by a ring of fire was preferable to her employer's brittle questions. How had she so poorly misjudged the woman? She had thought she had worked her way into favour all these years, but this was not a side of Mrs Moore she had encountered before. "I shall only be away the two days the shop is closed."

Mr Moore patted his mother's skeletal hand. "Come now, Mother, Miss Fitzwilliam is at liberty to spend Christmas as she pleases."

Mrs Moore delicately rubbed her forefinger delicately beneath her nose. "Very well. In the meanwhile, I expect you back at your station tomorrow. Seven-thirty, sharp!"

Chapter Six

Jim Buchanan

WOOLOONGILLY DOWNS, NEW SOUTH WALES, 16 DECEMBER 1853

6 PM.

From the wagon's seat, Jim surveyed the nearly three thousand sheep from beneath his hat brim. They milled nervously even though there was no imminent danger on this northwest corner of Gilly Downs, ten miles from the head station. Crivens! Those thick fleeces would be a welcome addition to this season's shear. A worm of discomfort wriggled through his gut. With such a successful clip on the horizon, it was one thing to get these purses-on-legs back to the station alive and in good health, but another entirely whether he would have the manpower to shear them all. Half his bloody shearers had scarpered earlier in the year to Echunga in the Adelaide Hills —lured by another whiff of gold. Much depended on the Elias Shipping Company's latest batch of emigrants. For the love of all that was holy, he would damn-well ensure this clip went right, even if he had to shear this lot himself.

Flicking the reins, Jim set the creaking wagon in motion again, squinting through the overcast gloom towards Wilkinson leaning against the iron hurdle of the make-shift yard. The barrel-chested Yorkshireman had adapted his years of cattle farming on the Yorkshire Dales to that of sheep farming in the New Holland bush.

"Best get on with counting them if ye plan to make the tally before dark," greeted Jim.

Wilkinson straightened, the neck of his shirt open to his belly button flashed a leathery tanned torso, and sweat-tightened curls of chest hair. A far cry from the pasty northerner who had given up his green, rented pastures in England to make a resourceful life for himself shepherding in this desolate corner of the world. Wilkinson raised the crook above his head in greeting, the fist of his rough, bush-dweller hands meaty around the wooden staff. "We'll be glad of your help, sir!"

A dog darted over, yapping as though warning him to stay away from her flock. Jim let out a high-pitched whistle, and the dog's ears flattened immediately as she slunk over, whining softly in recognition. Nevin and Wilkinson's isolated life was made easier and more pleasant by the company of Nipper, their working dog, named after her early instinct to nip at the sheep's hocks. Jim drew back the reins, and the giant bay's hooves crunched to a halt in the dry twigs and leaves. He stepped from the wagon, groaning as he stretched the stiffness from his knees. Ruffling the dog's grey-and-white-speckled ears, he laughed. "Who ye barking at, ye daft mongrel?"

Nevin stepped from behind a tree, halfway through buttoning up his trousers, his long legs gambolling eagerly towards Jim.

"Uncle Jimmy! Tell me you've brought some of Cook's oat biscuits? Bloody bush rats got into our supply night before last. Cleaned out the lot!"

All grown up, his nephew no longer led the gang of Barclay children on fishing expeditions now that he was a shepherd. The young man's wide-mouthed grin split his black beard, radiating the sunshine in his bones. Not even his shaggy, uncut hair could cover those family ears. Jim remembered his own youthful exuberance at this age.

Jim squinted at the square, bark-clad shepherd's watch-box, its roof weighted down by pegged logs. A sun-bleached sheet, once navy now grey, hung across the glassless window, the tatted weeds valiantly protecting the hut's interior from the sun's unforgiving gaze. As rustic as the home was, it offered a level of comfort not found in a domed, bark gunyah. The two men did a marvellous job of taking turns as watchmen from the small, weather-proof hut beside the yard while also keeping a good fire burning outside—both were excellent shepherds.

Jim glanced at the thick, grey clouds gathered above, and tipped his chin at Nevin. "You fixed the leak in the roof yet?" It was so bad his last visit he would have found better shelter under a tree.

"Aye, she's as tight as Wee Granny Mac's purse strings!" Nevin's chest collided with Jim's in embrace. His nephew's heavily muscled hand thumped him affectionately on the back, raising a cloud of dust.

He laughed, relishing the lad's sense of humour. "Speak no ill of the wee woman. She was kind enough to send ye each a new sheepskin to pad yer cots."

Nevin threw his head back laughing, his white teeth still youthfully intact. "Probably wrenched it from under poor Old Quill while he slept." He helped Jim slide a chest from the wagon's rear and, weighing it with an appreciative nod, plodded backwards towards the hut. As station manager, Jim visited all the shepherds, taking with him provisions and news. He was looking forward to a night with his nephew.

Wilkinson's sharp whistle jolted Nipper into action. "Best get this lot tucked in safe and sound before the storm comes. Blasted wild dogs have been on the scrounge again. These brainless beasts will make the easiest meal if they scatter at the wild weather."

Despite the threat of rain since sun up, the heavens held their bounty, and the cool of the evening invited deep calm and restfulness. With the sheep secured, Wilkinson threw more wood upon the perpetual fire before the watch-box, and took a seat on the logs around the crackling woodpile. Nevin's shadow ducked and weaved like a dancer around a Beltane fire as he prepared a supper of damper and kangaroo stew, while Jim fetched three bottles of ale from his personal supply chest on the wagon. The bubbling stew dripped into the fire, and the night came alive with the hiss of steam and sizzle of grease.

The cork squeaked as Jim pulled it from the bottle with his teeth and spat it into his palm. By all the holy saints! It had been a long, muggy day, and despite the ale's warmth, its yeasty charm slaked his hard-earned thirst. He smacked his lips, gasping. "Sweeter than Mary's milk is what this is." He held the bottle out to the two men. "While riding the wave of success, may we never meet a friend on the leeward side. May we be blessed with a bountiful clip because, by the holiest Mother, we've earned it."

"We've earned it," echoed the two men, and they clinked their bottles against his.

Dipping his chin, Jim sniffed. He stank of dust, sweat and smoke. "By, I'd do anything for a rinse in the creek back home," he said wistfully.

"Remember when Mr Singh stopped by, how the Barclay boys and I hunted for leeches in the creek?" Nevin's youthful tone lifted and sped up at the memory.

Wilkinson burped loudly. "What the devil d'you use as leech bait?"

"We flung our trousers on the bank, and lifting our shirts, offered our wee pink legs." Nevin chuckled.

"'Twasn't only yer wee pink legs the leeches took a liking to, if I recall?" Jim laughed. "Especially when ye strayed in a bit too deep."

Wilkinson snorted and slapped his knee. "Hellfire! I'd rather shite a hedgehog than offer me dingle-dangle to leeches."

"*That* only happened once." Nevin smirked and shrugged. "We'd sun ourselves on the grassy edge waiting for them to gorge themselves silly before dropping off our legs."

"So they were blood drunk?" Wilkinson's dirt-encrusted brow scrunched, wrinkling into grubby furrows, and he shook his head. "Never heard of such a tall tale."

"'Tis true! Every word," objected Nevin, waving his near-empty ale bottle about.

"Why d'you do it?" The broad-shouldered shepherd asked curiously.

"Mr Singh paid us tuppence a dozen."

"What he do with 'em? Cook up a curry with 'em?" The Yorkshireman's sunburnt brow wrinkled.

"No," explained Jim. "He'd sell them to the Rum Hospital in town for a ha'penny each."

Nevin's boots ground the gravel as he spun around. "*A ha'penny each*! We were robbed! We took such care to pop them in a jar filled with creek water, and seal the lid to prevent escapees. By God, we even wrapped the jars in wet sacking to keep the leeches cool and alive for their journey to Sydney Town."

Hooting, Jim stretched his legs out. "'Twas a worthy financial transaction for lads yer age. Didn't want ye getting too big for yer breeches, now did we?"

"Robbed!" muttered Nevin, shaking his dark head again.

He turned his attention back to lading, and handed Jim a scalding tin plate heavy with stew, topped with a generous hunk of torn damper. The thick fragrance of roo and potatoes made Jim's stomach growl, though he doubted it would compare to his Pearl's cooking. He dipped the bread into the thick, brown gravy and took a giant bite. Mother of saints, it was hot! With eyes watering, he swallowed down the pain with a mouthful of ale. Blowing on the next scoop, he fully appreciated the tender, gamy meat and crunchy damper crust.

They ate in silence, all attending the demands of their body before their need for conversation. Scraping his last piece of damper to mop up the last of the salty gravy, Jim sucked his thumb clean, and grinned at his nephew. "Not bad."

"Made it the way Aunty Pearl showed me. Secret's in the onions," said Nevin, winking. "How's my wee aunty?"

"She's with child—again," Jim said, as heavily as a judge reading out a sentence of execution.

"Oh," said Nevin, his gaze slipping to his lap. "Perhaps this time it will be different?"

"I pray so too, lad," murmured Jim.

Wilkinson coughed deeply and gathered their empty plates before disappearing around the hut's rear. Metallic clangs and sloshes of water spoke of his industry.

"I'll just check on the sheep, aye?" said Jim stiffly. He rose and headed towards the hurdled yard.

He and his Pearl had been married for eleven years. Although she begot a child easily enough, she had yet to deliver a live one. These days, he was too petrified to touch her. Was this a sign they were not meant to share this life together? He gripped the metal hurdle railing, still warm from the day's balminess. He had sworn he would not let himself go to her, no matter how many times she assured him. She had cried for a month the last time, and he dared not risk her going through that again. But one night a few weeks back, she had approached him in the dark, reaching for him. How could he refuse her the comfort when he needed it just as urgently himself? And now, her hopes were falsely inflated again.

He could not speak to her of his misery. What did she think of his silence? That he was against the notion of having a child? Christ, nothing could be further than the truth! But his life was too entwined with hers to imagine losing her. Nothing was worth that. Nothing. So, he chose the one escape he knew well, to head out into the bush again, his justification to visit the shepherds validated by truth. He searched the dark horizon, filled with sounds of life, the breeze breathing through the tops of the eucalyptus trees, the low-pitch hiss and screech of a quoll challenging a possum's nervous teeth-chattering. A violent shaking of foliage colliding with a pitiful scream cut the peace. Death was never far.

He squeezed his eyes tight. His last memory teetered on the other memories, piling up like a mound of scavenged bones at the back of the beast's lair. He remembered the last one well— too well—rain and wind hammering the bark shingles with such ferocity it shook several loose. He had scrambled to shift furniture and position pots and kettles to catch the ever-increasing drips from the wooden beams above while Pearl grunted and moaned in the bed, refusing to cry out. Catching leaks was constructive, something he could do to avoid his helplessness. He was unable to ease the struggles of the woman he loved too much. If he did not love her so, her agony might not have twisted his innards like a pitchfork loosening hay.

Afterwards, in the lantern glow, the sight of his Pearl curled in the bed, sobbing silently, was etched inside his skull like scrimshaw on a whale tooth. The memory folded in on itself like a paper bag, and he forced his eyes open so he would not remember. God damn the whole world! He thumped the metal railing, and the metallic rattle ricocheted into the night as the flock collectively jumped, their grey-shadows bleeding away from him with desperate bleats. He relished the pain in his hand.

Nevin sidled up, standing silently while Jim fought the shallow gasps forcing their way out of him. His nephew gripped his shoulder. "'Tisn't your fault, Uncle. 'Tis the way of life."

"Aye, 'tis my bloody fault!" Jim snapped, his chin quivering. "If 'tweren't for me, she wouldn't be going through it all again." He rubbed his face viciously, scrubbing away grief's thousand, tiny needles that pricked his eyeballs. "Christ!"

How could he face Pearl's da now? In the smoky gloom of The Sailor's Homecoming, he had promised his father-in-law that he would not touch her again—not after the last time. Mr Clementine had slammed down a pot of ale before Jim, the contents slopping like a wave crashing over a ship's bow, then dropped heavily in the chair opposite.

"Jim, my boy, let me tell you something for nothing. The older you get in life, the more you learn to hold on to what ya got. Stop chasing a young man's dreams. They only bring misery." The grizzle-headed dairyman tipped up his ale, draining half the contents before swiping the foam from his top lip with his arm.

Jim's ale sat untouched. A fat, black fly scurried around the rim, stopping at intervals to taste the foam with its pulsing proboscis. He stared at the insect, preferring to watch the thief steal his ale than meet his father-in-law's contempt.

"My Pearl's the only joy wot I got left on this miserable rock," said Mr Clementine. "Nearly took meself into the bush to have a word with me rifle's muzzle after her mother left. God rest her soul."

Jim chanced a glance. Mr Clementine's gaze on his own ale was unfocussed with the memories. He snapped his chin up, and the misery in his grey eyes slammed shut, his glare hardening like granite. "I'm warning ya. Subject my Pearl to the same fate as her mother, and *you'll* be the one speaking to the noisy end of me weapon. I won't have her taken from me like that just 'cause ya can't keep ya one-eyed snake out of her."

Stiffening, Jim drew his shoulders back. "Ye've no say over such matters. 'Tis my right as her husband." How dare he! It was bad enough he was yoked with his own guilt, but to have this old codger jump up and down on his nape was almost more than Jim could bear.

Mr Clementine thumped the tabletop, his wrinkled neck lurching forward, his growl low and ominous. "Ya forget who ya talking to there, my boy? Might 'ave earned my ticket-of-leave, but it don't do away with the fact that I killed a man to get 'ere." He tipped the remaining ale back, and slammed the pewter pot down with a smack of his lips. "You bring any 'arm to my Pearl, and I'll gladly take that tally up to two."

Jim had shoved his chair back with a dry scrape, the power and anger of a punch building between his shoulder blades. It would not do to strike the old bastard, especially not one who was family, no matter how disagreeable he was. He could not do that to Pearl. Old Clementine was a twisted, old husk whose every ounce of pleasure and gentleness had been wrung out of him over a lifetime. The miserable fool was only looking out for his daughter. It served no purpose to rationalise with him or explain that harming Pearl was the last thing he ever wanted. For the love of all things holy, he did not need unsanctioned marital advice from his father-in-law to know that the only way to protect her was to keep his distance.

But she kept inviting him back for more with her caresses in the night that promised he was the only man in the world she singled out for her attention. Her soft, sleepy breaths scented peach with brandy. Her gentle fingertips on his shoulder warm with desire. The bedframe's creak as she slipped atop him. Whispers as alluring as the pull of the blue open ocean. Her movements a dance, picturesque and desperate.

"Uncle—" Nevin's voice brought Jim back to the dusty paddock.

"Leave me be, lad," he snapped. Even if angry words did not eliminate his own agony, they at least might make the lad go away. He resisted the urge to rub his face again. He felt Nevin's gaze upon him, his sympathy, and he did not want it. His nephew's strong fingers gripped his shoulder tighter, and he nearly gave way to the strength of love in his boy's grip. A clasp that liquified his grief into something a little less miserable.

"I wish there was something I could do. Neither of ye deserves this." Nevin's voice deepened as it thickened.

"No. We don't. Christ, I'm tired of life shitting in me mouth then expecting thanks!"

"Remember what you told me after Da was killed?"

How could he forget? The sight of Nevin flung over Rory's bleeding corpse, killed by Major Winfield's careless bullet. The wee lad's pitiful wail signalling the moment he became an orphan.

"What was that?" said Jim.

"Ye promised to build yer future alongside me, with me, for me. And ye've done just that. Am I not legacy enough for ye, Uncle? Have I let ye down?"

Jim gripped Nevin's wrist, and the lad's grip on his shoulder firmed. "Christ, lad, no! Ye became my son the day me brother died. I couldn't be prouder of the man ye've become."

"Then I'll repeat what ye said to me all those years ago," whispered Nevin. "Yer difficulties are a raging river, and nowt can change its course except to let it flow past. I'll be right here on the bank beside ye 'til the waters calm, Uncle Jimmy."

Jim sometimes wondered what the chart of his life would look like had he chosen a life at sea. Would he be like Alby Church, carefree and with the liberty to move where the wind blew him? Would he still be aboard the *Elias*—as her captain, perhaps? It was almost laughable now, thinking back to his first few years as a powder monkey on the *Discerning*. The miserable, stinking conditions of the leaking forecastle cabin in a gale were preferable to the tempest of agony and rage of the last few years with his beloved Pearl.

Jim took a deep breath, the open bushland's aroma of tall grass and rich soil—the smells of home—eased the ache in his chest. He coughed twice before trusting himself to speak again. "I believe yer due to bring this lot back home early in the new year?" He waved a shadowy hand towards the stink of lanolin wafting from the enclosure.

"Aye. Might have to be sooner so as not to chance the dogs snatching any more of them. Squatter Shyling's paying bonuses this year to shepherds with the fewest deaths and highest lambings. Reckon Wilkinson and I are in with a chance."

Jim slung his arm around his nephew's tall shoulder. "If we set off tomorrow, we'll make it back to Gilly Downs in time for Christmas Day. Mrs Shyling's invited the whole bloody district to dinner. Ye may as well come and pay yer aunty yer respects, and make merry with the rest of us."

Chapter Seven

WEE GRANNY MAC

WOOLOONGILLY DOWNS, NEW SOUTH WALES, 16 DECEMBER 1853

8 PM.

Wee Granny Mac sat in Old Quill's cabin, watching the hearth still glowing from supper. The shimmer of rising heat was a contrast to the Scottish Lowland's bone-chilling mists seeping into her brother's croft so many moons ago. But with her feet currently afire and under attack from the gout, knee-deep Scottish snow sounded heavenly right about now. Pale lantern light danced across the singe-spotted rug and flickered across the pruned face of the old bastard at the table beside her. Christ! The look of him would make onions cry! Good thing she was partial to them.

75

Back when she first arrived at Gilly Downs, and Old Quill had probed about her real name, she had scowled at him before snapping, "If ye must call me by another name, then ye'll call me by the name my brother did—Grizzie."

"Grizzie," smiled Old Quill. "Ah, so you were Grace at your birth, I take it? Just like Mrs F."

Calling her this name was not Old Quill's only commonality with her brother. Both preferred raw neeps to cooked, both lauded her black sausage, and both had taken care of her in their rough-edged ways. Being cleared from her brother's croft by the laird meant starvation or emigration. In the end, her brother's attractive accounts of Port Jackson swayed her towards the latter —until the barmpot upped and died on her the week before their departure on the *Clover*.

Now, Old Quill's gnarled, liver-spotted hands gently placed the spoon in her clawed fingers. Her gnarled hands had finally succumbed to old age, limiting her independence, a stage in life that did not sit well with her. But Old Quill chatted amiably, seating the spoon-handle comfortably without so much as a hitch in his rambling monologue, or a sideways rheumy glance.

She swatted his arm away with her elbow. "Away with ye fussing, old man!" The trembling handle rattled against the tin bowl like a blasted cowbell as she scooped a dollop of chicken stew. Old Quill had thickened it with extra potatoes to prevent her from wearing the meal instead of eating it. She worked the tasty mush around her toothless gums, and inhaled the pleasant aroma of honey-slathered bread the old man had laid on the table for pudding.

Old Quill smacked his lips. "Ah, nice and salty. Just the way I liked it! Better than ye poisoning me with yer lettuce or canned black cherries."

"Ye'd never eaten so well in all yer life afore ye met me, ye old codger. 'Twas for yer own bloody good." She winced as the briny stew heated her insides, blowing fire through her veins to torture her already burning extremities. Despite his eternal fussing, she knew Old Quill kept the peace at home by complimenting her cooking, even though she no longer shouldered this responsibility. He had also silently taken over several of her chores, like clearing the fireplace each morning, and setting a new fire going for her.

"Keep calling me *old*, and you can see yourself to bed," he mumbled around a mouthful of bread.

"Ha! The last time ye flipped me in bed, yer poker barely warmed my hearth."

Old Quill's shoulders jiggled. "I only flipped you so as I didn't have to look at the mantelpiece while stoking the fire."

"Ye cheeky beggar!" She jabbed his forearm with her bony knuckles. "What makes ye think I fancied yer dried leather strap anyway?"

He chuckled again, and tapped his temple with a crooked finger. "Ah, but you see, darlin', I know the secret to make you want me."

He was right. He lured her to bed every night after supper with the same promise—to rub the fire from her feet with liberal doses of lanolin grease.

And tonight was no different. Old Quill worked the thick yellow grease into her feet with a milking rhythm, the cool of his skin against her hot, swollen feet and ankles soothing, like warm milk poured directly into a wound. Relief radiated up her calves, and she sighed. "That sawbones, Sykes can keep his fancy potions. Lanolin is the ultimate cure-all, as far as I'm concerned."

Old Quill caressed each misshapen toe, and ran his palms up her dry papery shins with long, slow strokes in time with his humming. His touch was more tender than any lover's, and she should know—more than one dog had jumped her fence over the years.

Her days, swaggering down the rutted path that crossed the

creek and led up that blasted hill to the shearing shed, were done. So, Old Quill had hammered a lean-to against their hut for her poddy lambs. Despite his best efforts, the old place gave an impression of affection and economical repair, though she was bleeding proud of his garden out the front, roped with yellow roses. A muffled bleat filtered through the thin wooden wall.

"Ye know, old man, I've had just about all life has had to offer—barring bairns."

Old Quill stopped humming, and snorted. "No way you'd have brought up a child, Grizzie. Christ, you can barely bring up phlegm!"

"Knowing your luck, our bairns would've been so cross-eyed tears would've run down their backs." She flicked her wrist towards the muffled bleating. "Fortunate I was sent those wee beggars, wasn't it? All fluff and knuckles, they are," she said gruffly, picturing the tight white curls of their heads butting her gnarled fingers.

"You're as tough as old mutton, Grizzie, fattening them lambkins for the table. Does it not pain you to kill them after all your care?"

She snorted back a thick glob of rheum, and swallowed. "Do it 'cause I have to, not because I like it. And 'tis not like I eat any of 'em myself. Besides, ye know well enough a sheep's main aim once in the world is to get out of it as fast as possible, wi' or wi'out my help—gormless creatures! There's ne'er grumbling around a table of bellies filled with roast." She shuffled deeper back into the lumpy pillows behind her. Providing fattened lambs for Cook up at the big house had been her crowning accomplishment since arriving in the colony. Determined not to be rendered useless or be a burden to Squatter Barclay, and now Squatter Shyling, she kept a rotation of a dozen creatures of varying ages —not a difficult achievement given the rate ewes abandoned their young. Was all part of the service, ensuring the station hands got a good daily feed.

She inhaled through her cleared nasal passages. Pity the sweet odour of garlic and herbs the old man had used to season the chicken soup was being drowned by the lanolin's stink. Old Quill talked of the old clearings back home, and what was to be done about the lairds. Bloody rob dogs deserved to fall down the stairs with their hands in their pockets! Back then, she had preferred solitary farming life of not seeing anyone else but her brother, nor leaving his allotment for months on end. There had been no other familiar faces with whom to exchange practicalities, complain about the weather, or share fragments of a day. Considering she favoured the company of beasts over humans, the isolation had not bothered her one iota.

She must be getting soft in her old age since she now enjoyed these evening conversations with Old Quill immensely—not that she would ever tell *him* that! They talked of the future, with some foreboding, and she was glad time would take her long before any of their prophecies came to fruition.

"Cooling down yet?" asked Old Quill, easing his hands off her feet for a moment.

"Aye, a bit. Don't stop."

He patted the top of her foot with a gloopy tap, then resumed his gentle rubbing. They talked of coming generations, of the old ways and the new. Old Quill's snowy brows clashed together like two ancient maggots at war. "Saw Clodagh return to the big house yesterday. Slunk in looking suitably sorry for herself."

"Hmph, just 'cause she was caught once doesn't mean she hasn't flattened a lot more grass in her time."

"Speaking of flattening grass, 'tis time I lay down my own old bones." Old Quill slipped the thick woollen socks over her knotted feet. Their padding made getting out of bed in the morning more bearable than pressing her swollen joints on the compact dirt floor. He wiped the excess grease from his hands with an old rag and dropped it beside the bed. Reaching for a stubby chisel from the bedside drawer, Old Quill scratched out a new notch on the wall behind. He had been marking their days together like this from the first night she shared his bed, and an intricate pattern of scored rows filled the entire back wall—much more satisfying than any of those fancy wallpapers up at the big house.

Shuffling up beside her, Old Quill's jaw cracked as he yawned, flashing his six remaining teeth, black and white like a row of broken piano keys. He sloughed off all his clothes—randy bastard always slept as bare as the day he was born. He was sight enough in this poor light, which was why she refused to open her eyes in the sunlit morn until he was dressed. He extinguished the lantern and lay back with a groan.

She wriggled over until her shoulder touched his, not that she would ever be caught dead doing so in daylight. The night had always brought down the barrier between them. It was easier to navigate what they had together in the dark. For over a decade, she had fallen asleep pressed alongside his bare, bony shoulder, and she was not about to stop now.

"Heard Father Blackwood's joining us for Christmas Day," Old Quill's voice was softer in the dark.

"Ye know he'll chance asking us to reconsider getting wed—as he always does?"

"You still not inclined to indulge him?"

"Not a dog's chance."

She breathed him in, this man of hers who smelled of sweat, dust, and wood smoke. The pillowcase beside her rasped as he turned his head, and she turned hers, their faces almost touching. His hot breath held traces of honey, ale, and rotten apples—she had smelled worse. By morning, his breath would be as sour as a peat bog—not that she minded since it carried the earthy perfume of ancient moss back home. She felt safe within this nightly monastery with him, where her heart was free to beat without remorse, without interruption until morning.

"Don't ye dare think about leaving this earth afore me," she whispered.

"Life isn't removed by death, Grizzie, it only appears so. I'm goin' nowhere without you." He patted her wrist, and left his hand covering hers.

"Good! I don't trust ye not to make a wrong turn and end up in Hell." She mashed her gums together with a satisfied suck. "Night, old man."

"Night, Grizzie."

GRIZZIE JERKED AWAKE, frowning at the night pressing in. What had woken her? A koala's grunt? A mosquito whining in her ear? Milady's ginger tom—whose fur matched the hair on her bairns' heads—caterwauling a midnight love song? She had always favoured cats, but she hated that one! Still, she dared not risk upsetting the evil blighter. Everyone back home knew that on Samhain, the *cat-sìth* would bless all houses that left a saucer of milk out for it, and those that did not were cursed by having their cows' udders run dry. She had even saved that wee Nessa's life by keeping her locked in her cabin aboard the *Clover*, despite seeing grown men come to blows over the wee black moggie's purported murder. Bloody fools, the lot of them! She had not dared risk the kitten's life with *that* lot. The wee minx disappeared during a ferocious storm off the coast of South America. Grizzie had hoped the cat would resurface once the ship limped into Montevideo, but she had not. At least a watery death was kinder compared to some.

Grizzie listened to the cabin's black air. No, it could not be a noise that disturbed her, she had as much chance of hearing as Old Quill's gammy leg had of running. Jesus, she had known warm nights before, when the hot air lay across her like a second, slick skin, but tonight, the evening sounds sucked into a collective breath as though keeping a secret, solemn and silent, holding their tongue in a language she could not speak. Though that could just be her deafness.

Easing onto her side, she wiggled her toes, grunting in relief to find them freer and less painful than earlier. Ha! She might even be able to shuffle to the outhouse in the morning without the old man's help. Fancy not being able to take a piss by herself! Beside her, Old Quill's moon-blue silhouette showed his hooked nose and sagging, open mouth. It beat him sleeping with his lips closed, his breath bursting from him like the blasted trumpets of Jericho. She closed her eyes, heavy with sleep. The old sod had better not wake her again tonight. Sighing deeply, she waited for slumber to descend, willing herself into darkness before his snoring started. She opened one eye. He usually shook the bedframe, snorting like an angry bull elephant when on his back.

"You awake, old man?" she croaked. Christ, her mouth was as dry as a lizard's belly. Too much bloody salt in the stew was what it was. Well, he could jolly-well rally and fetch her some water.

Old Quill did not stir. She lay her crooked hand on his wrinkly bare chest. His saggy skin was as cool as if he had been for a dip in the creek.

"Old man?" She shook him, and his head tipped towards her, his eyes still closed, mouth still slack. Dread crawled across her skin like the skittering legs of the nemesis huntsman spider that had crawled up her skirts in the outhouse. One firm swat had sorted that devil out but, deep inside, she knew there would be no remedy this time. "You bastard, you promised!"

She wheezed, the pain in her heart like a slowly sinking knife in her chest. Christ! Make it quick. A deep, low keening began in the pit of her stomach. Were she a sprightly lass, she might survive this agony, but she knew it was more than her aged body could handle—more than she wanted to handle.

Warm tears soaked her cheeks. "Wait for me, old man. I'm coming." The ache inside tightened, curling around her lungs like a cat's unsheathed claws. She lowered her head, resting her cheek on his cool chest. "The hardest life with ye was better than the kindest death," she whispered, closing her eyes.

The pressure in her chest released like a broken clock spring bursting free, and she gasped, opening her eyes. Aquilla Jacobs stood beneath the pretty arch of plaited twigs, ribbon and foliage curving over the old homestead gateway—the same archway she had helped decorate for Jim and Toby's weddings a lifetime ago. Quill looked thirty years younger with his black hair washed and sleeked back. She had not thought he even owned a brush! And what *was* he wearing? His suit was crisp with newness, not a crease out of line. He could very well be a grazier in this fancy get up.

Quill's shoulders drew back, and he gripped one open edge of his black jacket with carefree ease, tugging it smartly into place. He bowed deeply and, nimbly flipping the shiny black hat from under his elbow, popped it atop his head.

"Ye look like a bloody puffin!" She tugged the bright-orange kerchief knotted about his neck.

"You're quite a vision yourself," he chuckled, his dimpled smile so handsome with all his teeth in place.

She glanced down, frowning at her white, lacy gown. "What the devil are ye up to, old man?"

Beaming, he offered her his elbow. He stood taller than usual. "I'm here. For you."

Confusion swirled, and she gripped his bicep, her long, straight fingers curling around the sinewed muscle, firm with vitality and youth. "Where are ye taking me, ye silly clod?"

He patted her hand with long, lively fingers. "Anywhere you want, Grizzie. Anywhere you want."

He waved at the black carriage festooned with white lace ribbons, looking like bloody regurgitated unicorn cud. She squeaked in surprise as his strong hands gripped her waist, lifting her with ease. Plopping down on the seat with exasperation, she turned to scowl at him beside her. Over his shoulder, the usual Gilly Downs crowd gathered on the cottage veranda. Squatter Shyling, head and shoulders taller than the rest, raised one arm. Father Blackwood, with his arms crossed over his black, leather Bible, was smiling at her like a blasted cupid, all rosy-cheeked and cherubic. What had him looking so smug? And what the Devil was Elijah Barclay doing here—red whiskers ablaze? Beside him was Milady and all the children.

"Quill, what's happening?" she hissed. "Why's everyone staring?"

"They're here to say goodbye, Mrs Jacobs." He flicked the reins, and a puff of dust burst from the horse's rump as it lurched forward.

"Who ye calling *Mrs Jacobs*, ye dozy dolt?" She twisted in her seat again to stare at the receding crowd, the waving of hands and hats and handkerchiefs blurring the beloved faces she considered family. A trail of shoes bumped along in the dust behind the carriage.

Aquilla Jacobs, the man who had never said a single word about love, patted her knee. "'Twasn't the fear of our lives ending that haunted me as much the fear of not having you by my side for the next one. Only love gives us the taste of eternity, and by God, Grizzie Jacobs, do I love you!"

The horse clopped towards the thick blanket of mist that always found itself married to the creek in winter. Cool air prickled her skin. A soft ethereal breeze, never before felt, caressed her long, golden hair.

"Christ, we must be dead for ye to be sprouting such sentimental claptrap!" Sliding closer to Quill, she tightened her grip on his arm, torn between a desire to hold on to him, and a pulling urge to look back one last time. She was reluctant to leave the familiar behind. Ahead lay the unknown and, for a moment, a quiver of apprehension tripped down her vertebrae. Why could he not just take her home?

He tucked her under his arm as the carriage wheels clattered over the wooden bridge, the white cloud closing behind. She inhaled deeply as if she had risen from the deepest ocean, swallowing the familiar smell of him. It was as though she could read the scents on him, each telling a chapter of their lives together.

"Hush, Grizzie. For years, you've given me safe harbour, but you're the one in need of rescue right now. Let it be. I have you."

His eyes were dark, deep and hooded in a way that tightened some deep reflexive muscle inside her belly. No man had elicited *this* in her in years. The devilishly handsome charmer knew it too by that twinkle in his eye. She arched one brow suggestively. "Aye, ye have me, all right, Aquilla Jacobs. God's own eyes can see how yer now blessed with the vitality to butter my bread—and butter it well! I hope yer hungry."

Chapter Eight

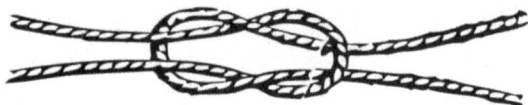

GRACE FITZWILLIAM

WOOLOONGILLY DOWNS, NEW SOUTH WALES, 25 DECEMBER 1853

Grace was drawn onto Barclay Hall's veranda by the festive buzz. She smiled at the light of happiness shining in so many pairs of eyes. It was wonderful to see so many familiar old faces, as well as new. She admired the long Christmas centrepiece with its red ribbon woven through the tangle of reedy eucalyptus stalks and gumnuts, and her mouth watered at the fresh mandarin oranges and mangos nestled in the wreath's foliage. The sweet scent of cinnamon spice from Cook's successful festive candles blended with the mint and honey tones of the eucalyptus leaf décor. With the sunken sun giving lead to the star-speckled night sky, the light from the oil lanterns and candles bathed the stretched table and its occupants in an enchanting glow. Seamus pulled out her chair with a dry scrape, and she sank beside Adelia.

Christmas dinner at Gilly Downs was a decidedly more raucous affair than Christmas in London, but Grace was in her element. She glanced over at young Moses Barclay seated on the other side of Adelia, his little head strapped in a great canvas sling. The youngster's blue eyes, marred black and purple bruising, scoured the groaning Christmas fare with such longing before lowering to his cup of beef bouillon. He picked up the two-handled bouillon cup adorned with soft yellow, red and lilac flowers. His lips reached out for the rim, not unlike that of a horse reaching for a carrot, and he slurped. Closing his eyes in evident rapture of the beef, onion and celery flavours, he swallowed.

Adelia smiled indulgently and, stroking his red curls, turned to Grace. "I hope you'll forgive a slurp or two? It's terribly difficult for him."

Grace patted Adelia's forearm. "Not at all. I think Moses is a real brick for joining us this evening." She picked up her own bouillon cup, humming at the salty liquid around the softened chunks of carrot and turnips. She leaned past Adelia, grinning at Moses and smacking her lips. "Delicious!"

The boy's giggle trickled into grunts of pain as he cupped his bandaged jaw.

Grace nudged her wrapped bonbon over to him, winking. "Here, take this for when you can enjoy sugared almonds again."

Moses's eyes widened as his stumpy fingers wrapped eagerly around the gift. He stuffed it into his pocket.

"This is for you too, young man, since you can't enjoy any Christmas pud today," said Victor Shyling from the table head. His giant index finger pushed what appeared to be a snuffbox across the white cloth to his stepson.

Moses inspected the painted scene of a young boy with a

pull-along horse trailing behind. He frowned, turning earnestly to his mother.

"It's a music box, sweetie. See here." She rhythmically wound the tiny handle on the side, and a tinkling rendition of *God Rest You Merry Gentlemen* began playing.

Moses's nostrils flared as he inhaled in delight, his bright, clear eyes wide with wonder at the new discovery. He turned the handle in uncoordinated motions, butchering the perfectly good Christmas carol. Momentarily drawn by the soft tinkly music, the rest of the table laughed.

Capitalising on the momentary lapse of conversation, Victor raised his glass. "A toast!" All eyes fixed expectantly, and a wave of glasses rose. "To old friends, may our years of friendship be multiplied again."

"To old friends!" repeated the crowd joyfully.

"And to new friends, may they become familiar faces of old," Victor boomed.

"To new friends!" Grace took a generous sip of the Penfolds Riesling, rolling her tongue around the fruity aromas of apricot, pear, and lime peel. It was sweet, delicious, and slid down far too easily!

Victor dropped into his chair, the wooden feet squealing on the veranda planking, his eyes darting eagerly to the slices of roast ham and pearly orbs of pickled onions on the platter before him.

The clamour of voices resumed their conversations, and Seamus slid his wine glass onto the table. "How many outposts do you have now, Shyling?"

Victor crunched a pickled onion, hastily swallowing to answer. "Four. Though, the Buchanan lad and Wilkinson are by far the most successful. Those men were destined to have the dust of this land in their veins."

At the mention of Nevin's name, Ruth jolted opposite Grace as though stung by a bee. The girl glanced at her giant, black-haired stepfather, her face taking on the look of a keen-eyed kookaburra spying a fat witchety grub as she hung on his every word.

"I've been meaning to send a hutkeeper out to them, so they can expend their efforts on the sheep instead of the trivialities of tending vegetable patches and boiling billies of tea." Victor's deep voice was melodic in its unhurried tone. "Thought perhaps Opal McDermott might be up to the task now that she's eighteen?"

If Ruth Barclay was a cartridge of black powder, her stepfather's words were an open flame. She detonated in her seat. "Oh, Papa, no!" Her ruby cheeks deepened like a glowing ember below her blazing flames of red hair.

Victor covered his surprise at Ruth's outburst by walking the caterpillars of his eyebrows towards one another in a deep scowl. "You don't think two hard-working men deserve a little help around their homestead?"

"Oh, no." Ruth flapped one hand. "I only meant, what about me?"

"What about you?" Victor slowly clasped his thick fingers together, wrists resting on the white tablecloth.

"*I* can be their hutkeeper." Unblinking, Ruth sucked her cheeks in.

Victor slid his gaze over to Adelia before drawing his attention back to his stepdaughter. "Opal is far better suited for the life of a hutkeeper."

Ruth stiffened. "I can do it!"

Victor leaned towards her, lowering his voice, "I've no doubt you can, young lady. But as Elijah Barclay's daughter, and my stepdaughter, it's not fitting to reduce your station to that of a hutkeeper. Besides, you're not old enough. Hut-life is no place for a young girl." His firm look and finite tone ended the discussion, and he turned to Seamus to ask about the Elias Shipping Company.

Grace offered the spirited lass and encouraging smile, but the bristling Ruth slid her eyes away, glaring at Opal's humorous protest down the other end of the table. "No Mam, don't!" objected Opal.

Grace perked up to hear Elsie McDermott's tale about her eldest daughter. "I recall the first time my Opal spotted Nevin showing the younger boys how to offer themselves up as leech bait in the creek." Elsie's brown eyes sparkled with delight in the flickering light.

"Mammy!" Opal's renewed objection was accompanied by a crimson flush.

"Hush you." Dorian McDermott laughed paternally. "'Tis my favourite story."

"Sweet Mary, Mother of Jesus," Opal mumbled, shaking her head and lowering her eyes to her lap as though she knew her parents would delight in dragging the story out if she protested.

Grace flicked her gaze to Nevin sitting beside Jim and Pearl. Nevin strained his dark head forward, his smile hidden by his thick whiskers. Pearl had no meat on her plate and was delicately sipping on a tumbler of cloudy ginger beer. Her pale face was tinged green along her jawline. Her round eyes—which Jim had once described as being as large and brown as a dairy cow— were uncharacteristically marred by dark rings. Poor thing! Grace had felt exactly the same way about meat when she was with child.

With their intrigue whetted by the young girl's reaction to her mother's story, the other diners' offered Elsie their full attention.

"She couldn't have been more seven since it weren't that long after we arrived at Gilly Downs," said Elsie in her soft Irish lilt, her heavy black bun bobbing as she gestured. "There I was, plucking a chicken for supper, when young Opal pulled on my apron, declaring she'd seen a boy down by the creek without any clothes on." The table erupted into laughter. Opal laughed too, though she kept her eyes cast down, shaking her head. Elsie continued, "I didn't quite know where to look, but knowing of children's' curious minds, I asked how she knew him to be a boy?" Elsie turned to look at Opal's bowed head, her dark eyes sparkling with mischief. "And blinking at me through those blessed dark lashes of hers, she innocently replied, *course he's a boy—he has short hair and a tongue at the end of his belly.*"

Dorian exploded, slapping the table to reinforce his merriment, the cutlery jangling.

Grace smiled at Opal in sympathy. Poor girl. At least she kept her humour about her. Opposite, Ruth's red eyebrows tightened in a scowl, and her glower at Opal carried the spark of a thousand flints. If she glared any harder, her vitriol might just set Opal ablaze! Grace twisted her head back to Adelia, nudging her with her elbow.

"Are Ruth and Opal no longer friends?" she asked from the corner of her mouth.

A breathy laugh escaped Adelia as she shook her head. "Good Lord! You've just opened Pandora's box, my friend."

Grace tipped her head. "I have?"

"My Ruthie and Opal have had their sweet friendship soured by their mutual affection for Nevin Buchanan."

"Oh, dear." Grace winced. "That can't be easy for any of them. How old is Ruth now?"

Adelia stretched her lips. "Fifteen, going on fifty! Far too young to be caught in a rivalrous triangle."

With appetites and thirst satisfied by Cook's banquet, tables were emptied and chairs pushed back along the wall, clearing the veranda for dancing. Grace watched the merriment from the bank of chairs near the front door, where she sat resting before her promised dance with Edwin. Grace smiled at Edwin leading Emily in a jig. Both the same height, their natural comfort with one another synchronised their movements, allowing them to simultaneously talk and gallop about. Our Em's golden curls bounced in time with the music, and her straight white teeth flashed in the lantern light as she laughed. Whatever her brother had said was clearly weighted with mischief if that dimpled smirk of his had anything to say about it.

Grace turned her attention to Nevin. Fuelled by Cook's potent whiskey-stewed prunes and heavily brandied Christmas pudding, the wide-eared shepherd's energy was insatiable as he careered up and down the veranda, towing along a ruddy-faced Ruthie. For all her wealth and station, Adelia's coppery-headed daughter had as much subtlety and femininity as a newborn giraffe—all long legs, knobbly knees. Through a patchy web of freckles, she beamed up at Nevin, shrieking as he whirled her around in time with the McDermott's piano and violin. She looked so happy.

Beside her, Billy nursed a bulb of brandy, his long fingers curling elegantly around the glass. Those same fingers had guided each of her children into this world, and she had the sudden urge to grip them tight and never let go. Instead, she nudged his shoulder with hers. "We could have done with another woman or two. These poor lasses can't catch their breath with all the demand."

Billy's brown gaze darted from her face to his brandy then out into the night. "I'm a physician, not a brothel madam. I couldn't have helped with that." His voice cracked on the last word, and Grace studied him in her periphery.

It was not like the doctor to be so defensive. Then again, it was not like him to be so crapulous either! She had always cherished the ease with which Billy confided in her over the years. It made her reciprocation effortless too. Though, something troubled her friend tonight, and she was positive it was not too much drink.

"Out with it, my friend. Your secret is as plain as a joey's bulge in a kangaroo's pouch."

Billy dragged his long black fringe back with unsteady

fingers, his unfocussed eyes narrowing in concentration. "I've no idea what you're talking about."

"Billy Sykes, you look as shifty as the day you caught that trout in the Yorkshire Dales. Then, after cooking it over an open fire, told me it was still alive."

Billy snorted. "Aye, and I told you if you didn't believe me, to stick your finger in its mouth, and I'd prove it was."

Grace held up her index finger, examining it closely. She pointed to a tiny white scar just above her nailbed. "And then you snapped its jaws shut and sunk its teeth into me, you cheeky beggar!"

"My da always said lassies were easy to catch like that, and he was right." He winked.

Grace thumped his shoulder, laughing. "I should've known you'd be up to your old tricks, but I got you back with those leeches in your bed."

He nodded, his lips pursing quirkily, his nod impressed. "Aye, that you did."

"Right, so tell me what you're hiding this time? Or that lovely, fat python inhabiting the woodshed might slip between your sheets when you're not looking."

Billy's weathered cheeks greyed, and he wore a conflicted look. He was terrified of snakes. Would he risk a snake in his bed to keep his secret? It had to be a good one! He looked at her for the length of three heartbeats, then shook his head. "She's not worth it."

Grace straightened her spine. "She?"

Scrunching his eyes and rubbing his nose, Billy grunted. "I meant, *it's* not worth it. 'Tis a business matter."

"You said *she*. Come on, Billy, who is she?"

He tipped back his brandy and took a mouthful. "No one you know, and not anyone you're likely to get to know."

"What, are you the court jester now, bamboozling me with your riddles? Is she a patient?"

He shook his head. "Even if I named her, you'd not know her."

"Ah, so there is a her!" Grace hissed secretively, gripping his bicep and shaking his arm. "Out with it. Who?"

Billy snapped his lips shut with exaggeration and, swaying in his seat, made a negative noise in the back of his throat. "She's a … supplier. A medicinal supplier."

Grace slapped her hand to her chest with an embellished gasp. "Don't tell me, she has two heads? A convict? Is married?" She clapped her hand to her forehead. "No, Billy! Not a married, two-headed, convict! What *were* you thinking?"

His lack of denial eroded some of her humour. There was no way Billy would embroil himself in something so scandalous, would he? His reputation as a brilliant doctor and healer would be tarnished forever if he was foolish enough to dabble in a dalliance—and he certainly was no fool. Grace studied her childhood friend from beneath hooded eyelids. The man had embraced bachelorhood with the piety of a monk. Why the sudden appearance of a woman in his life, but more importantly, why the secrecy? He plainly did not want news of his acquaintance with her spread about town.

"She could be all that and more for all I care—if her potion will do what she says it does." For all of his nonchalance, his words were weighted with a pain she had not heard before.

"And what's that?"

"Save Erin Hicks' life."

A double-handed grip of fear latched onto her spine. "I thought she was well? The babe too."

"Mrs Hicks survived her latest ordeal. It'll take a miracle to prevent catastrophe."

"And this mystery business acquaintance of yours holds the answer?"

Billy's lips tightened, and he shrugged indifferently. It was clear that nothing more of his boozy blunder would see the light of day.

Before she could extract the answer from Billy, Victor leaned back in the other seat beside her, and grimaced as he rubbed his bulging stomach. "Dear God, I ate far too much!" He belched, and his black-whiskered cheeks bulged. "Damnation! Feels like Satan's clawing up from the fiery pit of my stomach. Shouldn't have had that last mince pie."

Billy frowned at Victor's sherry glass resting untouched on the windowsill behind. "That half bottle of sherry wouldn't have helped matters," soothed Billy empathetically. "Especially not atop all that dancing."

Victor belched again. "What tonic do you suggest to remedy a roiling gut, Doctor?"

"An easy amble and small sips of milk should restore some order," said Billy. He leaned back, stretching his own belly. "Perhaps I might join you for a stroll to the kitchen? Hopefully, Cook didn't use up all the milk in the custard."

Ha! The canny doctor was making his escape. Never fear, she would learn of his mystery woman eventually.

Victor lumbered to his feet, and Billy unfolded beside him, nodding at the grazier to lead the way.

Victor bent to kiss the top of Adelia's head. "My apologies, sweetheart. I'm not the young man I once was. That Christmas pud has me beaten. It's in the best interests of my overindulged stomach to follow doctor's orders." He dipped his head at the seated men. "Care to join us, Captain? Father?"

Father Blackwood rose eagerly, his own generous belly stretching out before him. Seamus stood in one smooth motion, the bulb of his own brandy glass neatly balanced in one hand. He gave Grace a triumphant grin at finding himself successfully on his feet. She had not seen him this inebriated since his overindulgence at The Sailor's Homecoming after his fight with Alby Church. At least there would be no flare of jealousy or flying fists this evening. Then again—she flicked a quick look at Opal stewing behind the piano where she sat with her mother, hammering out the tunes that had her admirer dancing with another girl.

Biting her bottom lip and shaking her head at her husband in amusement, Grace angled her head as he kissed her cheek, his familiar stubble prickling. The homely smell of him blended with eye-watering brandy fumes as she looked into his swimming, blue eyes.

"Back in a jiffy," he said with careful annunciation. He pressed his warm lips to her ear. "Keep looking at me like that, my heart, and I'll have to whisk you off for a private word. Of all I plan to do to you tonight, *nothing* will be in moderation."

By the Bells of Old Bailey! She had forgotten how emboldened he became when bolstered with a bit of Dutch courage. She flicked a guilty look at Father Blackwood, but he was laughing at the antics of the group of single shepherds and station hands around a bonfire at the centre of the gravel carriage circle. Sliding a coy look back to her husband she shivered as goose flesh rippled down her neck in anticipation. She traced a slow, teasing finger across her open décolletage. "Promise?" She tittered as his nostrils flared.

"Shameless," he slurred, stumbling off the veranda's last step, and gripping Father Blackwood's arm. The four gentlemen ambled past the crowd of station hands, all laughing amiably, cheeks aglow with drink.

Nevin deposited a panting and sweaty Ruth in the vacant chair between Grace and Adelia. Emily sauntered over, her glass replenished with cloudy elderflower cordial. She sank into Billy's vacated chair on the other side of Grace, her rosy cheeks bulging in a grin at Nevin's theatrical bow.

"Ladies," greeted Nevin. A shout of laughter by the bonfire caught his attention, and he jolted down the steps, withdrawing a small leather book from his back pocket. "Righto, lads. Who's up for a spot of poetry?"

Grace chortled. "I thought young Nevin had an aversion to anything reading or writing related?"

"Not entirely." Ruth sucked in a deep breath and blew it out slowly. She swiped her wrist across her glistening hairline. "He's not that fond of writing, but he has realised the use in reading. I've been lending him books from our library for the last year."

Edwin and Jim also joined the ranks on the lawn as the young men about the fire groaned in unison. What a pity Toby had been unable to make it, thought Grace. He would have loved the camaraderie. Still, it was marvellous news about little Dorothy's arrival.

Undeterred by the men's protests, Nevin recited a poem with alcohol-induced earnestness. *"The brown bowle. The merry brown bowle. As it goes round about – a!"* He exaggerated the last word, and the men bent double with laughter. Grace giggled helplessly at their unbridled mirth.

The drunk poet swayed, scowling at his unappreciative audience. "Yeah, no, you've gotta let me get thi-sh out." His earnest plea brought more raucous laughter from the men, but they soon settled, leaning forward, elbows on knees.

Tilting the book towards the firelight with inebriated slowness, Nevin spoke with a thick tongue, "Fill. Still. Let the world say what it will. And drink your fill all out—*a!*"

Two men collapsed from their log seats onto the stony driveway, rolling and clutching their sides. Others used their sleeves to wipe tears from their cheeks. Grace covered her face, burying her own laughter.

Nevin persisted louder. "The deep canne. The merry deep canne. As thou dost freely quaff—*a!*" Realising that the men found great hilarity in the word *a*, Nevin emphasised it with a theatrical flourish of his hand. Caught up drunken hysteria, the men were barely able to listen through their howls of laughter.

Nevin staggered, holding the little book close to his face, chin tipped up and hand still braced in the air. "Sing. Fling. Be as merry as a king. And sound a lusty laugh—*ha!*" At this last exclamation, Edwin tackled Nevin's legs, bringing him crashing heavily to the gravel to join his comrades in their side-splitting merriment.

Leaving the bonfire revellers to their boyish wrestling, Grace shook her head good-humouredly, and turned as Ruth pleaded, "Please, Mama, persuade Papa to let me go. I'll take *much better* care of Nevin than Opal will."

Adelia slid a sideways glance in Grace's direction. With a look of mutual understanding, Grace knew it would take no time for Nevin to fall for Opal's raven-haired beauty and charm when isolated away from the head station—it would not be only his billy can she warmed at night.

Adelia grasped her daughter's hand. "Come now, Ruthie—"

"Don't call me that. I'm not a child anymore." The freckles on Ruth's alabaster cheeks darkened as she snatched her hand back.

Straightening her back, Adelia inclined her head. "I know you aren't, but Papa is correct. Opal has been in training for this position since she was a little girl. And if Papa ever caught wind of your affection for Nevin, he would ship you off to England."

Ruth dipped her chin to her chest, a tear dripping from her chin. Sniffing indelicately, she turned to her mother, her lips in a rigid line. "Perhaps it's time for me to leave Gilly Downs? I'd much rather an adventure of my own choosing than to be exiled by my stepfather."

Grace reached for Ruth's other hand and squeezed. "Ruthie —Ruth, my darling, your papa is a good man. He only has your best interests at heart. He shan't be exiling you anywhere."

"Perhaps not," sulked Ruth. "But I can't stay here. I couldn't *bear* watching those two together."

Grace sighed. Ah, young love! So innocent, so unformed, so

inexperienced, yet ever so enchanting! Patting Ruth's leg, Grace gentled her advice. "Without making myself out to be an old crone, it's my aunt duty to caution you about the despair and suffering that can emanate from these situations. I know you're eager to experience love, but you're young. *So* young. You've time."

Ruth narrowed her eyes and pouted. "How old were you when you married Uncle Seamus?"

"Positively *ancient* compared to you, my darling. Twenty."

Ruth swivelled in her seat. "Oh please, Aunt Grace! Take me back to town with you. I'll do anything you ask of me. Run errands. Scribe letters."

Emily leaned forward. "Now that I've become Mrs Moore's first hand, she might have an opening for another apprentice seamstress."

Ruth's eyes widened. "Oh, that's even better!" Her long, speckled neck swivelled expectantly towards her mother.

Adelia nodded. "I'll need to speak to Papa about this. It'll take all my powers of persuasion. He's always had firm ideas about how the boys fit into Gilly Downs' future, but he'll be the first to admit that he's at a complete loss about what to do with you girls. He's never been keen about having you expensively educated, only to afterwards be expensively amused in leisure. The prospect of an apprenticeship works in your favour, but you shan't be going anywhere until after the next shear. I need your sharp eyes to help me class the wool."

Ruth swung round to face Emily, her earlier scowl now a scintillating smile. "How exciting!"

Shaking her head in amusement, Grace panned across the veranda, her gaze freezing on Pearl Buchanan sitting alone in the far corner. Despite the warm evening, the young woman had no more colour in her cheeks than earlier. Grace patted Ruth's knee. "I'll leave you and our Em to sort out this new life of yours while I pop over and keep Mrs Buchanan company."

Grace rose, and Ruth slunk into her empty chair, snatching our Em's hand. "You've a double bed, don't you, Em? I don't take up that much room."

Emily flicked a look at Grace before raising one brow at her friend. "When Eddy sails for London in the new year, you'll be able to have your own room."

Grace's stomach flopped over. Perish the thought! She waggled her finger at Emily and Ruth. "Not so quick, young ladies. Nothing has been decided yet about when or where Edwin will be going."

Adelia stood and looped her arm into Grace's, lowering her chin to her daughter. "Aunt Grace is right, Ruthie. I won't have you making Eddy feel a stranger in his own home. You two keep your good ideas to yourself for the minute."

Ruth, leaning back against the house and folding her arms, added, "Just think, I could chaperone you and your lovely Mr Moore at his mother's dances."

Grace slowly swivelled her head towards Emily, who in turn scrunched her nose and glared at the red-headed girl beside her. "Ruthie!" she hissed.

"Emily Elizabeth—" Grace injected a tone of caution. "You *know* what a stickler Cappy is for proper order. You shan't be going to any dances without his permission."

"But Mamam, what if he says no?" Emily wheedled. "Don't you always say it's better to ask for forgiveness than permission?"

Grace chortled. "Sometimes, yes, but not with Cappy, and not for this matter. He's a good judge of men. I'd like him to meet Mr Moore first."

"But you met him at supper the other night. Didn't you like him?"

"He was a perfectly mannered gentleman, but that was in the company of three women. Let your father meet him, and if he approves, you shall have both our blessings."

Emily bounced from her seat, and handed Grace her untouched drink. "Very well, I'll go and tell Cappy to expect a visitor in the new year then." She dragged Ruth up by the hand. "Come on, Ruthie, he might find it harder to say no if you're there."

Grace was about to caution her daughter that now might not be the right time with Seamus's current level of inebriation when Adelia tapped her elbow. She met Grace's eye, and tossed her head in Pearl's direction. "I'll join you in cheering up Mrs Buchanan. Poor creature is as miserable as a bandicoot. No one should look that unhappy on Christmas Day."

Grace lowered her voice. "Jim told me she lost another one a few months back, but that she's with child again."

Adelia sucked in a sympathetic breath. "Poor dear. Why can't men learn to leave well alone."

Humming, Grace leaned in, whispering, "I rather got the impression it was *she* who did the pressing. Jim's more than miffed with himself."

Grace and Adelia's skirts swirled about Pearl's legs as they sat on either side of her. An unbidden memory arose of the first time Grace had found herself seated beside Adelia at the governor's ball with the cantankerous Widow Crunk frosting the air between them. That old battle-axe had died many a year back, and this time it was not a miserable, young grazier's wife Grace was consoling, but her dear friend's wife.

Grace offered Pearl the glass of elderflower cordial, and the petite, dark-haired woman took it with a cautious smile. "Thank you, Mrs F."

"Did you manage to eat anything?" Adelia asked kindly.

"Just some damper dipped in gravy." She raised the sweetened drink to her lips, but her nostrils flared before the glass even reached her mouth, and she lowered it to her lap again.

A raucous burst of laughter around the campfire pulled Pearl's attention. Grace studied Jim, Nevin, and Edwin laughing and yelling over one another about who would be quicker at climbing the windmill down by Jim's cottage. Nevin snatched the bottle of rum from Jim and tipped it up to his mouth.

Grace tittered and shook her head. "No one will be climbing anything if they drink much more." Her laughter trickled as Pearl stared at Jim, unblinking. Grace leaned into her line of vision, and smiled. "Jim told me of your good news."

"It's only good to some." Pearl's voice was thin in the warm night air. "My da's threatened to shoot Jim if any harm befalls me." She lowered the glass to the floor, and folded her arms across her belly. "It'd be bad enough losing another little one without losing my husband too."

Adelia patted Pearl's shoulder, her voice firm with reason, "Come now, my dear. Fathers can be funny creatures when it comes to their daughters. I'm sure he shan't *actually* shoot Mr Buchanan."

"Mrs Shyling's correct," added Grace. "Men have an inherent need to bandy these things about, much like a mob lobbing rotten tomatoes at some poor soul in the stocks. Pointing out the rot of their argument before they have chance to put their throwing arms into motion is the quickest way to disarm them."

"Da shan't need disarming if Jim's not here." Pearl sniffed.

Grace waved her arm at the drunken campfire dwellers. "The drink might have carried him off tonight, but he'll be back in the morn—feeling rather sorry for himself, no doubt."

"I'm not speaking of the drink." Pearl tipped her head back and sucked in a deep breath. "Jim's threatened to run off to the goldfields to prevent putting me in any further predicaments."

Grace tutted gently. "If there's one thing I know about Jim Buchanan it's that he's as loyal as a mast is straight. He'd never forsake you or the little one like that."

Pearl murmured into her lap. "He forsakes me every time he rides off into the bush."

Adelia huffed in exasperation. "Come now, Mrs Buchanan.

Such is the life of a station manager. He's required all about the property, not only at the home hearth. All this self-pity isn't doing you *any* good."

Grace winced. Her friend's practicalities were overshadowing Pearl's grief. Only another woman who had experienced the loss of a child, unborn or otherwise, knew that it was not as simple as shaking out a dusty carpet and getting on with it. Even twenty-three years past, the memory of her first child, of her own pains and fear, had folded into the corner of her heart, and lived there like a hard pebble, a reminder, forever.

Mr Potts, the neighbouring grazier, shuffled to a halt before Adelia, one plump hand extended. Grace glanced up at the man who had headed the jury at her trial for Chittenden's murder. The girth of his waistband had clearly swelled alongside his prosperity, despite now being a widower. Still, he had been kind enough back then, and his gentle tone now still carried consideration. "Mrs Shyling, may I have this dance?"

Adelia tittered like a schoolgirl. She might be able to dip and dag sheep as well as any man, but the London society debutant, buried deep within, always came to the fore whenever she was asked to dance. Rising gracefully, Adelia regally inclined her head in acceptance.

Good! It would give Grace a minute to have a word with Pearl in private. She swivelled in her seat, and took Pearl's leathery-palmed hand. "I know no one speaks of these things, but I'm awfully sorry you've suffered a lifetime of loss. I too lost my first babe, and then when I lost my Elias, I released my sanity to escape the agony."

Pearl's chin trembled. "How did you find it again?"

"My husband and children promised to help me find my smile again."

Pearl plucked her hand back. "I've no such luxury. My husband runs off the minute I try to speak to him of it." She twisted her face away, swiping a thumb under her eye.

"He's hurting too," said Grace gently. "He's like a bear released from its cage—prepared to tear out the heart and lungs of anyone who would harm you. But there is nothing for him to fight in this battle, nothing he can watch for or protect, so he fights himself. His helplessness is crippling him."

"He can barely look at me," Pearl's voice warbled. "It's as though his love of me is a weakness he can't afford. Doesn't want to afford."

"That's not true. Jim loves you!" Grace placed her hand on Pearl's knee, her fingers sinking into the thick cotton fabric. "None of us can predict if tomorrow will be better than today—"

"Or worse," interjected Pearl.

Grace hesitated, then slid her hand over Pearl's folded arms that maintained a tight grip on her torso. "Be kind to yourself, Pearl. We can't know if this time will be different. We can only be hopeful that it will."

Would Billy's mystery potion would work wonders on Pearl too? There would be no answer to this tonight, but she resolved to ask him once he regained full control of his faculties.

THREE DAYS LATER, with the revelry over and all evidence of it cleared away, Grace stood hand-in-hand with Seamus in the graveyard on the hillside behind the shearing shed. The pink horizon brightened the grey sky, highlighting the two newly scored patches of earth laying side-by-side. Her husband's long fingers fitted perfectly around her hand, and she tightened her grip as the rich, loamy dust of the recently turned dirt coated the back of her tongue. Two achingly familiar names were scratched like scars into the temporary, white, wooden markers, *Grace Jacobs* and *Aquilla Jacobs*. They would always be Wee Granny Mac and Old Quill to her.

Seamus gently squeezed her fingers. "Penny for your thoughts?"

"I never knew I shared the same first name as Wee Granny Mac." She pointed to the new graves, their elongated shadows purple in the orange dawn light. "And when did she and Old Quill wed?"

"They didn't," said Seamus.

She tightened her forehead and hummed. "I know Father Blackwood never relinquished his determination to have them married, but if they never did the deed, how come her marker carries the Jacobs name?"

"Father Blackwood said that since Old Quill never gave up on his quest to make her his wife, he thought he would honour the man's final wish, and have them laid side-by-side as husband and wife." Seamus chuckled. "Not as though she can return and change her tombstone." As though agreeing with him, two kookaburras above turned their calls for breakfast into jagged laughter.

Grace tittered. "I wouldn't put it past her."

She pictured another far-off grave nestled on a rocky shoreline, overlooking the glacially formed valleys and rugged snowy peaks of a windswept archipelago. Gilly—dear, dear, Gilly—her storm lantern, who turned a lonely, miserable night into a velvety cocoon of safety in the *Discerning*'s forecastle cabin—despite its belching odours and lack of comforts. Whenever trouble came her way, he always had creative solutions that eluded others. He was that friend, found only once in a lifetime, who had stayed with her as a warm and steady light all these years. Gilly had proven to her what loyalty and love looked like.

Pulling gently on Seamus' hand, Grace drew him around the remaining headstones, her shoes crunching to a halt in the bark and leaf crumbs before each familiar name. She let the wash of memories cleanse her sorrow. *Rory Buchanan*, Jim's older brother and Nevin's father. Shot and killed by a stray bullet in a shootout between bushrangers and police. His sacrifice was not in vain. He had left Jim the gift of raising a son. The only son he might ever know since it seemed Pearl was unable to have one of their own. Nevin was a good man—Rory would be proud of him.

Elijah Barclay, Adelia's first husband, father to her five children, and pioneer of Gilly Downs. He had made sure she was in good hands—even on his death bed, he had not steered her wrong. Victor Shyling was a loyal husband and wonderful father to the children. Meandering through the other headstones, her thoughts trailed to Elias, buried with Seamus's parents in St Pancras—the same place Grace had experienced that happiest of days, marrying Seamus. With its dry, thirsty earth and sunburnt grass, this wild graveyard was a world away from the ordered, mossy churchyard where their son lay. "Do you still feel our boy? Our Elias?" Grace asked softly, her words carrying off on the breeze like a secret.

Seamus paused, then his nostrils flared as he inhaled. "I do."

"What does he feel like?"

Seamus did not reply right away. He rolled his wrist, and it clicked. Shuffling his feet in the crumbling dirt, he faced her and rested his hands on her shoulders. "He's just *here*. It doesn't feel good or bad. Just here, like you are."

Grace pressed herself against her husband, squeezing her eyes tight against the press of tears. Her Luckenbooth brooch dug into her chest as she tightened her grip. She breathed him in, gathering strength from the familial, citrusy scent of him. "Oh, my sweet Elias. I feel the same. I hope he's found peace. Not a day goes by when I don't think of him."

He wrapped his arms around her. She let the high chirps of cicadas, industrious in the summer morning air, surround her as she shared Elias's presence with the only other person on earth who felt what she felt, whose heart beat in time with hers.

"I imagine this is how it'll feel when Eddy leaves," she said.

Just as the cicadas never stopped singing, neither did life. A reminder that history moved forward, even though it sometimes tugged her back. A reminder to cherish the now. A reminder to keep looking ahead. Gilly's wise words echoed from the past. *You can build on the deeds that have happened or put the catastrophes behind you and begin again. 'Tis the way of life, offering a new chance every day.* It was time to give Edwin his chance at life.

"You mean … you're letting him—"

"Yes. I know I can't keep him pinned to the home hearth forever. I just thought I might've had another year or two at least."

Seamus swayed her gently, like he used to when rocking the children in comfort. "We'll only need to look up and know we're under the same sky as our boy." He pressed a kiss into the top of her head and chuckled. "And hope that he's not too busy enjoying the adventure to pause and give us a thought once in a while."

A horse's whinny echoed across the valley as though impatient to press on with today's homeward journey. She could remain here all day, melded against Seamus's torso, the two of them one. Detecting his flinch of awareness, she peered over her shoulder at our Em and Eddy ambling through the long crispy grass on horseback, towing two saddled horses. Reluctantly, Grace stepped back, and slid her hand into Seamus's again. "Ready to head home?"

"I am if you are, Dulcinea." The permanent groove down his cheek deepened with his smile.

THANKS FOR READING *CHRISTMAS AT GILLY DOWNS*. I HOPE YOU ENJOYED IT AS MUCH AS I ENJOYED WRITING IT. I'D LOVE IT IF YOU COULD PLEASE TAKE A COUPLE OF SECONDS TO POP A REVIEW ONLINE ON THE STOREFRONT WHERE YOU PURCHASED THIS BOOK.

ALSO BY EMMA LOMBARD

The Gold Hills Series

Continue on with the Fitzwilliam family saga from The White Sails Series. Follow in Emily Fitzwilliam's footsteps as she makes her mark on the world. Head over to the author's website for more information and developments of this series:

www.emmalombardauthor.com/the-gold-hills-series

OTHER BOOKS FROM EMMA LOMBARD

Discerning Grace

The White Sails Series, Book One

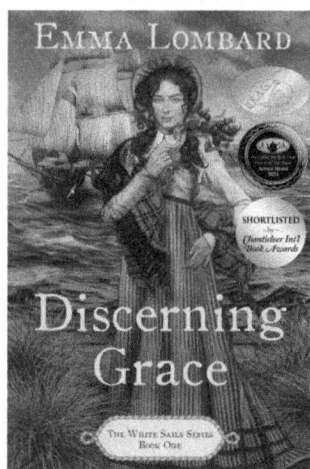

A rollicking romantic adventure featuring an independent young woman, Grace Baxter, whose feminine lens blows the ordered patriarchal decks of a 19th century naval tall ship to smithereens.

Grace on the Horizon

The White Sails Series, Book Two

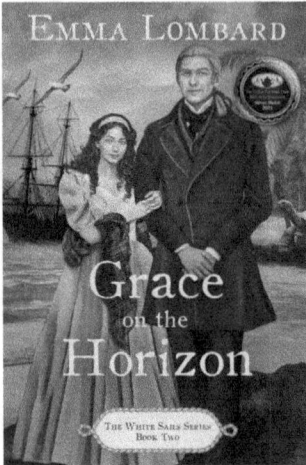

Continue Seamus and Grace's romantic sea adventures. Secrets and rumours abound as these two headstrong opposites try to expose the saboteur aboard their exploration vessel.

Grace Arising

The White Sails Series, Book Three

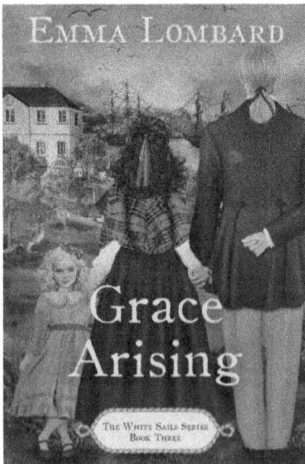

A new ship means a new adventure. With Seamus gravely injured, it's up to Grace to see the crew and her family to safety. Can she reach the New Holland wool market ahead of their competitors, and in time to save Seamus's life?

Christmas at Gilly Downs

The White Sails Series, Book Four: Christmas Novella

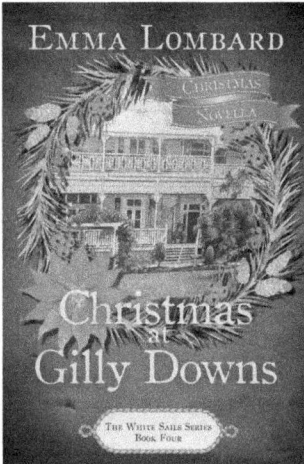

Jump forward ten years to see what the beloved characters from The White Sails Series are up to as they prepare to reunite for Christmas at Gilly Downs.

CPSIA information can be obtained
at www.ICGtesting.com
Printed in the USA
LVHW042201120722
723217LV00006B/264

9 780645 105865